"[A] POIGNANT AND HEART-WRENCHING STORY OF LOVE AND LOSS."
—*Abilene Reporter-News*

"In this exquisitely crafted, ultimately uplifting novel, K. C. McKinnon beautifully captures the poignance of growing older, the comforting joys of friendship, and the glories of love in its many guises."
—*Poteau News & Sun* (OK)

"This deeply moving story is filled with friendship, joy, and sorrow that will leave you smiling through your tears."
—*Romantic Times*

"*Candles on Bay Street* is meant to be read in one sitting—preferably on a rainy day in front of a roaring fire. It is a touching story of what happens to baby boomers and flower children as they age."
—*The Tennessean*

"In a beautiful story of love, relationships, and loyalty, Sam, Dee Dee, and their other friends show us what really matters in life, even when everything isn't going perfectly."
—*Lancaster Sunday News* (PA)

"Irresistible."
—*M*

By K. C. McKinnon:

DANCING AT THE HARVEST MOON

As Cathie Pelletier:

THE FUNERAL MAKERS
ONCE UPON A TIME ON THE BANKS
THE WEIGHT OF WINTER
THE BUBBLE REPUTATION
A MARRIAGE MADE AT WOODSTOCK
BEAMING SONNY HOME

WIDOW'S WALK, poems

A COUNTRY MUSIC CHRISTMAS (Editor)
THE CHRISTMAS NOTE (with Skeeter Davis)

CANDLES ON BAY STREET

a novel by

K. C. McKinnon

BALLANTINE BOOKS • NEW YORK

Copyright © 1999 by K. C. McKinnon
Illustrations copyright © 1999 by John Hafford

All rights reserved under International and Pan-American Copyright Conventions. Published in the United States by The Ballantine Publishing Group, a division of Random House, Inc., New York, and simultaneously in Canada by Random House of Canada Limited, Toronto.

Ballantine and colophon are registered trademarks of Random House, Inc.

"My Girl"
Words and music by William "Smokey" Robinson and Ronald White.
Copyright © 1964 (Renewed 1992), 1972, 1973, 1977
JOBETE MUSIC CO., INC.
All Rights Controlled and Administered by EMI APRIL MUSIC INC.
All Rights Reserved. International copyright secured.
Used by permission.

www.randomhouse.com/BB/

This edition published by arrangement with Doubleday, a division of Random House, Inc.

Library of Congress Catalog Card Number is available from the publisher upon request.

ISBN: 0-449-00555-0

Manufactured in the United States of America

First Ballantine Books Edition: October 2000

10 9 8 7 6 5 4 3 2 1

This book is for my mother, *Ethel O'Leary Pelletier,* who is fighting a strong battle, and winning. And for my father, *Louis Pelletier,* in memory of those childhood days along the St. John River.

For *Brian LeBlanc* (my old college pal at the University of Maine at Fort Kent), who left this planet in 1976, when a drunk driver ignored a red light. And for his son, Brian, who was still unborn at the time, but who is now the very image of his dad. (Just days after Christmas in 1996, when I was lying in bed with what must have been pneumonia, I called upon Brian's memory to give me an idea for a story. This is it. Thanks, Bry. I miss your wicked smile.)

For *Augusta Ann McKinnon O'Leary,* my grandmother, who was born above the Allagash Falls, a site now gone to wild bushes and old dreams. I hope she's proud that I've chosen her maiden name for my pseudonym.

The town of Fort Kent, which sits on the St. John River, up at the tip of northern Maine, a place I dearly love. There is no Bay Street there. And I intentionally invented other streets so as not to give reference to any real house. But most of the physical elements in the book actually exist.

This book is also dedicated to all my Quebocois and Acadian ancestors, and to my Franco-American cousins, Quebecois, Acadian, and Cajun.

CANDLES
ON
BAY STREET

Sam's first wheels

ONE

"Every time you light a candle, an angel is born."
—DEE DEE MICHAUD, SPRING 1997

She was the childhood sweetheart I wanted to marry, but didn't. I blame General Motors for this. In 1982, when their new line of sleek Corvettes came off the assembly line, Bobby Langford bought one, a shiny gold, the color of the sun. And he looked so good sitting behind the wheel that Dee Dee Michaud fell head over heels in love with *him,* instead of me. There I was, standing at the curb and about to make my big move. The rest, as Neanderthal man might say, is prehistory.

I don't remember not knowing who she was. Hers is the very first face I can pull up when I flip back through the flimsy pages of my memory. She was part of my history, my family folklore, my roots: At times, it seemed as if she were a part of *me.* We were both two years old when she moved in next door, accompanied by Estelle and Marvin Michaud, who were known around our little town of Fort Kent, Maine, as "older parents." They had just bought the two-story Victorian next door to us at 204 Bay Street. I'm told that we met for the first time, officially, at my third birthday party a few weeks later. I can't remember this, but I have the pictures as proof. Even then she was ravishing, a two-and-a-half-year-old flirt, her party hat canted to one side of her head, wheat-colored curls exploding from beneath the rim. And in her eyes a bright mischievous fire that I thought would never go out. When we were five years old we took a bath together, in a big galvanized tub in the backyard. That's a hot photo I've been carrying in my wallet since the seventh grade, when I slipped it out of my mom's scrapbook, unbeknownst to anyone but me. Ross Cloutier was the only person who knew about the picture. "What would you say if I told you that I have in my wallet a picture of Dee Dee Michaud naked as a jaybird?" I asked. We were sitting at the edge of the potato field, on the outskirts of town, smoking Salem cigarettes and getting sick to our stomachs. "I'd tell you pigs could fly," Ross answered. I didn't bother to prove him wrong. I told myself it was because I was defending Dee Dee's honor. But the real reason I didn't show him the picture is that I'm sitting in the galvanized tub, crying my eyes out with embarrassment, while Dee Dee is dancing like a dervish, silver drops of water cascading down her back.

This has been the story of our lives.

When we were in the third grade Dee Dee beat up Vincent Cyr for beating *me* up. She was taller than me in those days. I hadn't yet started "sprouting up," as my mother predicted I would, an act that sounded terrifying to me. I would lie in bed at night and imagine myself looking like a large, radiation-ridden potato after the "sprouting" was over. But it seemed I had no stomach for Salems *or* fighting, in those days before the sprouting could occur. So Dee Dee fought my battles for me. When she returned the comic book Vinny had taken from me, I should've been embarrassed that a girl had come to my rescue. But I wasn't. "Here, Sammy," she said, "I think you dropped something." I looked up into those blue-gray eyes, deeper and bluer than the old swimming hole in the St. John River, and they were so sincere that I really *believed* I'd dropped the comic book after all. That was her power. That was Dee Dee.

In the fifth-grade talent show we were Bogey and Bacall in *Key Largo*. We fought about it for almost a month, right up to the night of the performance: Dee Dee wanted to be Bogey. It was the only time I never gave in to her.

Our freshman year of high school she was expelled for a week, for using profanity and smoking cigarettes in the bathroom. Her mother asked me to talk to her, so I did. "Your mother says you're running with some very wild girls," I said to Dee Dee. "Would you please introduce me to them?"

We formed a band our sophomore year, called the Acute Angles, because all four of us had geometry together. Dee Dee sang, I played lead guitar, Ross Cloutier played bass, and Brian LeBlanc played drums. We even managed to get a few gigs in town, but then Brian moved away and we couldn't find the heart to go on without him. Yet my greatest concern in those days was finding a way to get Dee Dee to stop the "buddy" thing and get straight to the sex. Otherwise, I feared I might die. On my tombstone would be the words: *Here lies the only male virgin in the Class of '82.*

A month before we graduated from high school Dee Dee started dating Bobby Langford. His parents were divorced and living in Connecticut, so they'd sent him north to the wilds, to live with his grandparents, thinking it would be good for Bobby. It was disaster for *me.* On the morning of our graduation, Dee Dee jumped into the passenger seat of my truck—a 1954 Ford pickup, an inheritance from my Grandpa Thibodeau that had taken me months to restore. On the drive to school, I decided to make my move. I would do it with humor—humor was what Dee Dee loved best. I'd be Woody Allen. I'd tell her,

"Listen, I know we've been friends. Hell, we've been Bogey and Bacall. But maybe it's time we were something more. I tell you what. This time, I'll let you be Bogey." But before I could say anything Dee Dee showed me her engagement ring. "It's a secret," she said. "Nobody knows, so don't tell. Okay, Sammy?" I didn't wonder where Bobby got the money for a diamond ring *or* the Corvette. He was making trips to Connecticut twice a month and a lot of good pot was suddenly going around the streets of Fort Kent, Maine. I looked at the ring. "O Great God Cannabis, thank you for your rewards," I said. I thought it would make her laugh, but it didn't. "Don't believe rumors, Sammy," was all she said. "Talk is cheap in small towns."

The very next day after our high school graduation—and much to the disappointment of her parents and everyone who loved her—Dee Dee packed her suitcase. Then she and Bobby and the sun-colored Corvette sneaked out of Fort Kent during the night. I heard from her two weeks later, when I received a picture postcard of a huge ball of string sitting above the words: *Visit Jennings, Louisiana, Home of the World's Biggest Ball of Twine.* On the back she'd scribbled these words: *Dear Samuel Louis Thibodeau. Ain't life a hoot? Love, Dee Dee.*

The next we heard she and Bobby Langford had gotten married. Mrs. Estelle Michaud, Dee Dee's mother, crossed the hedge that separated the

5

Michauds' yard from ours and came sadly up the steps and into our kitchen to tell my mom the heart-breaking news. She didn't even bother to stop, as she usually did, to pick up any candy wrappers that might have blown into the yard, or empty pop cans that might have rolled in off the street. She didn't bother to pinch the dead leaves from around the flowers she'd planted in narrow beds along the hedge. Instead, she came directly into my mother's kitchen, the screen door slamming behind her like a bang of reality. "That crazy girl has finally done it, Margaret," I heard her tell my mother. "That crazy girl has gone and ruined her life." I was sitting with one leg up over the side of Dad's easy chair, count-ing the seconds until my first semester at college would begin and my life could be saved from the most complete and utter boredom ever wished upon an earthling—now that Dee Dee was gone from next door—but this got my full attention. This turned life interesting again, for I knew right away who *that crazy girl* was. I came to stand in the doorway, lean-ing in just enough to catch Mrs. Michaud's words, and that's how I learned that the love of my life, Di-ana Catherine Michaud, voted Biggest Class Flirt and Prettiest Girl for four years straight, had married the man behind the wheel of that golden chariot of a Corvette. "She's just a baby," Mrs. Michaud said, wringing her hands and looking generally miserable. A week later I got a second postcard, this time from

6

Mankins, Texas. On the front was a picture of an enormous shoe: *Home of the World's Largest Cowboy Boot,* the heading read. On the back she'd written: *Dear Sammy. I'm so glad to be out of school and finally learning things about the world. Love, Dee Dee.* I pinned the postcard to the wall over the desk in my bedroom, next to the first one she'd sent, the ball-of-twine wonder. Then I took out the acceptance letter I'd received earlier that year from the University of Maine at Fort Kent, the small college in my hometown, and I reread all the words carefully. Some folks love to travel, it's true, but I knew then, a short time after graduating as valedictorian of Fort Kent High School's Class of 1982, that I would stay in my own town to finish college, aiming for a degree in science and biology. Then I would go off to vet school in Boston—as close to home as possible—for the four years it would take to complete a doctorate of veterinary medicine. But I would come home to my roots, and open a small animal practice in Fort Kent, where there was none. Like a lot of New England males I've known in my life, I'm the kind of man who stays close to hearth and kin. There's something in this northern Maine soil that has held me firmly to it. I should have known back then what this meant: A crazy girl who is wild as the wind wants a boy who is just as wild. Yet the unfairness of it all overwhelmed me. I couldn't compete with Bobby Langford by driving around in Grandpa

Thibodeau's truck. A 1954 pickup against a new Corvette? What woman besides Grammie Thibodeau would turn down the 'vette? Bobby Langford wasn't much at all without that car, but cars have a lot of power. Let's face it. Who would remember James Dean if he had died in a rusting, dented Volkswagen Rabbit? That silver Spider Porsche did it. My eyes filling with warm tears I never wanted anyone to see, I looked up at the two postcards again: *Ain't life a hoot?* Dee Dee had asked me. I tried to imagine her sitting atop the world's biggest ball of twine, or lying flat out on the toe of the largest cowboy boot, but the images wouldn't come. My only regret in life up to that short point of eighteen years had been that Dee Dee Michaud never slowed down long enough for me to *tell her* that she was the love of my life. I looked back down at the acceptance letter, and the catalogue newly arrived from Boston's School of Veterinary Medicine. I touched the tip of my index finger to each one. "There's the rest of your life, Sammy Thibodeau," I said aloud. "Get used to it." How could I have known then about life's tricks, about those smoky mirrors and false doors, one of which would bring Dee Dee Michaud home to Fort Kent and back into my life again? I couldn't. Just as Dee Dee couldn't know that her shaky marriage to Bobby Langford wouldn't last. In 1987, one year after I would graduate *summa cum laude* from the University of Maine at

Fort Kent, word went around town that Dee Dee had opened some kind of crafts shop in Wyoming— which sounded like the *other* end of the universe from northern Maine. The world spun on.

In February of the following year, Dee Dee's father died of a heart attack. I didn't come home from Boston for his funeral. I had an exam that week and vet school was tough. But Mother phoned to say that Dee Dee hadn't changed much. Now that Mr. Michaud was gone, Mrs. Michaud was making plans to move in with her widowed sister. She would rent out the house at 204 Bay Street. Mother would miss her old neighbor of so many years. So would I. Somehow, the notion of Dee Dee's folks still next door to mine had kept her memory alive for me. Before she hung up my mother said, "Oh, Sammy, I almost forgot. Dee Dee's eight months pregnant."

A month later, in March of 1988, two full years before I moved back to Fort Kent and opened my own practice, Mother wrote that Dee Dee Michaud had had her baby, a son she named Martin. No one seemed to know if Bobby Langford was passing out cigars. The news of the birth was followed months later by news that Bobby had gotten a good job working on the Alaskan pipeline. I imagined that he and his gold Corvette had headed north together, toward the Land of the Midnight Sun. After that, no one seemed to know anything about Dee Dee Michaud anymore. Months passed, and I woke up one day to realize that I'd heard nothing from her, or *about* her. The ties that bind seem to have been finally severed. I imagined that the gossips were busy back in our hometown, digging for details of her life. But I was busy, too. I had my final and hardest year of vet school yet to live through. And, oh yes, I had asked a vet student named Lydia Newhart to marry me.

Ain't life a hoot?

To this day I have never bought an automobile from General Motors. It's just a matter of principle.

At my clinic, long after everyone has gone home, I still allow myself to think about Dee Dee. First loves die hard. If it's almost twilight, her memory comes more easily: that late afternoon in the summer of 1976, when we were both twelve, the summer we learned all the words to "Fernando." It was our favorite song that whole year long, a hit by the Swedish group AßBA. Lying on our stomachs that summery day, searching for crayfish in the murky water under rocks, Dee Dee turned to me and said, "I want to be AßBA when I grow up, Sammy." I scoffed. "You can't be a whole band, idiot," I told her. I was just beginning to realize that I would love her all my life, and that's why I had begun to call her

10

idiot, and *monkey,* and *nitwit.* She was changing, too. The tomboy in her could turn soft and girlish with just a quick flash of expression. The tomboy in her was surfacing less and less. And there I was, locked in my skinny body which had started to grow tall without filling out, a body that would soon be pumping enough testosterone to fill the rock quarry out on Morin Road. Just then Dee Dee started to sing, a song about freedom fighters crossing the Rio Grande by starlight, the air around them alive and brimming with passion, fighting for liberty at any cost. Dee Dee, singing "Fernando" for the millionth time. Suddenly, she turned, skipped a rock out across the water. "I want to be a revolutionary, Sammy," she said. "I want to be like those people in the song, fighting for liberty under the stars." She stopped talking and looked over at me. "Kiss me, Sammy," she said. "With your tongue and everything. I wanna know what it feels like." Looking back, I know now that what I felt first that day was sadness. We were being taken away, purloined by time, our bodies changing without our permission. I could feel the day lurking just at our heels when our innocence would be wrested away forever. Why couldn't we stay right where we were, with our moms putting cold glasses of milk and warm cookies on the kitchen counter for us to find? With our sexuality still buried deep enough that it wouldn't hurt us?

"Listen," I said to her. "You been following me around too much lately and it's starting to get on my nerves." I said it to hurt her, only sensing in my growing bones that the day would come when I'd lie in my bed at night, aching for just the sight of her, knowing that she was on her front porch, right next door at 204 Bay Street, with Bobby "Octopus Hands" Langford hanging on to her as if she might evaporate. "You're never gonna be anything, anyway," I told her. "You're a nitwit." And then I climbed to the top of the little hill to get away from her. Funny how that day stays fresh in my memory: I replay it over and over again. Sometimes, I'm sitting in the office at my clinic, looking down at some lab report, when her twelve-year-old face suddenly materializes in my mind's eye. Or I'm cleaning dead leaves out of the downspouts when I hear her words, coming back at me. Maybe she, too, sensed what was happening, that our safe world was changing. Or maybe she knew that my anger at her wasn't real, that it was the only language I was equipped with then. After all, I was only a gangly boy whose body was jutting toward manhood. She had simply flopped over on her back and stared up at me, her blue-gray eyes the color of that northern Maine sky, her thick hair that had already turned from towhead to brownish blond splaying out about a face that would evolve into that of a beautiful woman.

"Hey, Fernando!" Dee Dee shouted up to me. "Can you hear the guns, baby?"

To this day I have a huge poster of ABBA hanging on the wall, behind my office door. It keeps me focused on the important things in life.

The clinic

TWO

I saw seven golden candlesticks.
—REVELATION OF ST. JOHN

Fort Kent, in the uppermost reaches of northern Maine, is a good place to raise a family, and Lydia and I knew that we wanted a family. But first we would work to see that our new veterinary practice had grown healthy enough to support us both. As Fort Kent had no vet clinic at all, we didn't think that would be too difficult to achieve. We would get the business of pet owners from all the towns around the St. John Valley, as well as those from across the St. John River—which formed the international boundary—in Clair and Edmundston, New Brunswick. So we bought the old Pinette house, just three streets over from where I grew up on Bay, in an area that had been zoned commercial. We set about restoring the downstairs into a perfectly workable animal clinic, the upstairs into a two-bedroom, comfortable home. In the few years since we'd opened the Northern Maine Veterinary Clinic our dreams seemed to be coming true. If things kept up, we'd be starting our family and settling down to middle age, to worry about teenage adolescence, and then the high price of college tuitions.

Fort Kent itself is a place of heritage, where French is still spoken in many of the valley homes, especially by the older members of the community, a French passed down to them from Quebecois and Acadian ancestors. Sadly, the younger generation, one raised on television and computers, has all but given up their parents' first language. Even with celebrations given each year by the genealogical society, celebrations in which Franco-Americans come from many states to honor their individual surnames of Marquis, Cyr, Levesque, Paradis, Desjardins, LeBlanc, Hebert, Ouellette, Nadeau, Perreault, Gagnon, Pelletier, Michaud, Belanger, Jandreau, Levasseur, and others, the young were more interested in watching the latest Tom Cruise movie or listening to Hootie and the Blowfish. Older members of the community were doing their best to restore French as a second language where it had, until the sixties, been a *first* language in most homes. But they were fighting a losing battle. The new generation of Franco-Americans in northern Maine saw themselves as simply *American,* and maybe that was best.

But French could still be heard spoken in any restaurant, or bar, or grocery store, almost as often as English. And you could order ployes at Doris's Cafe, buckwheat pancakes prized by the early Acadian settlers from Nova Scotia. The Canadians who lived in the houses that dotted the border, on the opposite side of the St. John River, spoke English as a second language, if they spoke it at all. This is what Lydia, born and raised in Boston, found most intriguing about her new home. She had even taken it upon herself to learn what is known as *valley French,* a patois that had changed a great deal from the original French that left France almost four hundred years ago.

Lydia felt at home in this unique little corner of the United States. She had always dreamed of living in the country, even as a small girl growing up in a Boston apartment building. Her love of animals, and of seeing them run free in wide-open places, had instilled in her the belief that she would have a farm one day, after she grew up to become a veterinarian. Asking her to marry me was more difficult than asking her to move north to the end of the road in Maine. I still wasn't too steady on my feet when it came to women. After all, I hadn't taken the time to find that first girlfriend back in high school, thanks to my being overwhelmed by the charms and graces of Dee Dee Michaud. And when Dee Dee finally flashed that engagement ring at me the day she agreed to marry Bobby Langford, I had decided that women were too unpredictable. I would concentrate on my studies instead. And that's what I did. I just didn't know that in my last two years of vet school, Lydia Newhart would be sitting in the chair in front of me, as intent on learning all about animal parasites as I was. She was pretty, in that natural way, long brown hair and hazel eyes, curvy yet athletic. She didn't tell me until months later that she had noticed me, too, and thought I was the only good-looking guy in the class. Granted it was a small class, but knowing this aforehand would have made my asking her out that very first time a bit easier. But I did find the nerve, and Lydia accepted. The epitaph on my tombstone would have to change: *Here lies a man with a smile on his face.*

By the time we decided to marry, I already knew that the move to northern Maine would be a dream come true for Lydia. We made preparations for that day. I took extra courses in large-animal husbandry, knowing that with all the valley farmers, with their numerous cows and horses, I could expand our clinic possibilities greatly. This would mean bouncing around on bumpy back roads in my new pickup truck. But after four years in Boston traffic, in wet Boston winters that blew in with a mighty vengeance from off the ocean, I couldn't think of anything I'd like better. And I'd be home where I belonged.

The clinic itself was something to be proud of. Lydia decided that since the building had once been someone's home, it would be a good idea to keep it "homey." So she papered the walls with rose-colored paper, with small roses on the two-inch border that ran around the top of each room. We left the hardwood floors just as they were, wide pumpkin pine boards that came to life beneath a new coat of varnish. Lydia put a few throw rugs on the floor, to add warmth to the place. In the waiting room she placed vases of whatever local flowers she could find: wild cherry blossoms in the springtime, flowers from our garden in summer, and goldenrod from some farmer's field in the autumn. Each Christmas she decorated with holly from Pelletier's Florist on West Main. We wanted our clients to feel at home in our clinic. After all, in a town as small as Fort Kent, with fewer than three thousand souls, we were all neighbors. And while Lydia and I entertained very little upstairs, in our living quarters, we saw just about every Fort Kenter, sooner or later, downstairs at our animal hospital.

Even in a town as well rooted in the past as Fort Kent there is change. Buildings that have been around for decades burn, or are torn down, altering the face of the town. Older residents slowly disappear from the streets, take up new residence in one of the town's two graveyards—Catholic or Protestant. And the next generation moves in to fill their shoes. This is life. Two years after I came back to Fort Kent, my father died. Mother tried to live on in the house on Bay Street without him, for three more lonely years, but then she gave up and bought a Florida condo, where two of her best friends had already retired. I hated to see her go, hated to see the house on Bay Street up for sale, but that's what happened. Mom needed the money to last her through her old age. And I had already bought land just outside the town limits, fifty beautiful acres, and hired a contractor to begin the building of what would be my and Lydia's dream house, the home where we would eventually raise our family. So I couldn't afford to buy the old house on Bay Street. And besides, what would I do with it? I already had plans for where I would live and die, on that hard-earned fifty acres. So the house on Bay Street sold to a family from Portland. "Why do they call it *Bay* Street when we're nowhere near the ocean?" Lydia had asked on her first visit to my childhood home. "You're starting to sound like a tourist," I told her. The truth was that no one really knew why *Bay* Street was not *River* Street. Wishful thinking on the part of some old-time settler, most likely. But, of course, no ocean also meant no whining, fussy tourists clogging up the summer streets and roads. The tourists we got in Fort Kent were mostly the hardy souls who had trekked north for spectacular nature and down-home wisdom, not lobster and caviar.

It's a difficult thing, seeing your childhood home being lived in by someone else, another family's laughter echoing in the big rooms, another family's nicks and scrapes being etched into the bones of the place. The Victorian house next door, at 204 Bay Street, where Dee Dee Michaud and I first met, had been vacant for several months. The family who had rented it from Mrs. Michaud had eventually moved out, and no one else had moved in to replace them. Word of mouth was that Mrs. Michaud was asking too much rent. Whatever the reason, the house sat joyless and empty. And then Mrs. Michaud died. People disappearing. We read her obituary in the paper: *Survived by one daughter, Diana Catherine Langford, 33; and one grandson, Martin Langford, 8, Jackson Hole, Wyoming.*

I tried not to look at either house on those days when I found myself in my truck headed out to that part of town. The grass had grown tall on the lawn at 204, its black windows staring forlornly at the street. How many warm summer nights had I spent, as lovesick as Romeo, peering out my own window at Dee Dee's organdy curtains, wondering what thoughts were swirling in her head as she slept, wondering what she looked like in the shower, wondering if she ever thought of me in the same way, not knowing that time would soon hurl us toward our futures and we would both be gone from those houses. I wish I had known then how quickly it would happen, wish I had paid closer attention to the seconds that were passing. But, like most young souls, I thought youth would be mine forever.

No one seemed to have much information about Dee Dee after her mother moved down to Bangor. Once Mrs. Michaud passed away, we wondered if we'd ever see Dee Dee again. She had long ago given up on silly postcards, at least where I was concerned. I suppose this isn't surprising. We grow up, we grow away from our memories, and the world spins onward. But as Lydia and I did our duty in keeping pets healthy in Fort Kent, Maine, in neutering and spaying and vaccinating, I couldn't help but wonder if Dee Dee Michaud ever thought of me. Or of those glorious sunshine days of youth that we spent along the river, evenings in my basement as we practiced for some talent show, or learned some new song for our little musical band.

Mostly, I didn't think about her. Life kept me busy. Animal husbandry kept me working long, contented hours. And now, our future home, the foundation of which was just going into the earth on Gagnon Road, kept me totally preoccupied. Lydia and I had drawn up the plans ourselves, four large bedrooms upstairs, one downstairs, with a nice sturdy patio overlooking the countryside. Our dream was coming true. The outer shell would be up by autumn, and then, in the spring of the following year, we figured we'd have enough money saved up to finish the inside. We'd be living in our dream home by the summer of 1998.

Dee Dee's name came up once in a while. My old pal Ross Cloutier, who used to be in our band, the Acute Angles, was still in Fort Kent, teaching history at the high school. He and I sometimes got together with our wives for a beer at Bee Jay's Tavern, which sat at the mouth of the international bridge. You could sip a beer at Bee Jay's while looking out the window at the lights twinkling in Canada. "A real international experience," Ross called it. And then Ross and Amy divorced and Ross started asking me out for a beer, just the two of us. An old song playing on the jukebox would prompt Ross and me to talk about our crazy days of innocence. "If we formed a band today," Ross asked once, "what would we call ourselves? The *Obtuse* Angles?" It was good to have him around. He was still part old hippie, born too late for those Abbie Hoffman–Angela Davis days of protest, but a staunch defender of man's natural right to smoke a little pot now and then, grow his hair down to his shoulders, or at least as long as the Fort Kent school board would allow. And then Ross met Vickie Perreault, who had moved back home from New Hampshire with a degree in English, and was now teaching at the high school as well. And it was back to the four of us, Ross, Vickie, Lydia, and I, walking down to Bee Jay's Tavern for a beer, the snow crunching beneath our boots if it was winter,

23

dead leaves scuttling in the wind behind us if it was autumn. On some of those nights, if I wasn't careful, I could hear Dee Dee's laughter trailing along with us, on these streets of our youth, voices coming out of the stillness of the movie theater, or wafting down from the ski slope, a distant laughter I believed was lost to me forever.

Then one bright spring morning, with tourists milling about the town office, hoping to buy a fishing license, with kids in line in front of the brand-new McDonald's, waiting to buy a Big Mac, with Lydia taking care of the line of clients at our clinic, I got into my truck and turned it toward the west end of town. A farmer's Holstein was down and didn't seem interested in getting back up. So the farmer had called me in a panic. About the last thing I cared to do that day was minister to a sick and possibly irate cow, and I had my mind on just that as I drove down Elm Street and turned onto Bay, knowing that at the end of Bay I could turn left again—a shortcut to West Main, and thus the road leading out of town. As I passed 206 Bay, my old house, I made myself look at the signs of new life taking place there: a blue car in the drive, strange flowers with large faces growing all along the hedge, a hammock under the old maple. There was even a new color to the shutters: black instead of green. It was then that I noticed movement next door, at 204, men inching across the lawn carrying a sofa. I slowed, then pulled up to the curb for a better look. A moving truck was parked along the upper side of the house, its back doors open, its belly full of furniture and odds and ends. I noticed a boy's bicycle against the steps leading up to the porch. The movers reappeared, ready for another load.

"Someone must have bought the house," I said to myself. I had long ago decided that seeing the house full of strangers would be better than seeing it sit empty forever, crabgrass and weeds careening about the yard, the curtainless windows looking sad and forgotten. I was just about to pull away, remembering the sick cow, when I saw one of the movers jump up into the truck and pass a large picture down to the man waiting on the ground. I've no idea what made me look at this picture, but I did. The second man accepted it, then turned with it in his arms as he carefully carried it across the lawn. It was a framed poster, five feet long and three feet wide, a huge, monstrous poster of AđBA. I watched as man and poster disappeared inside the house. I looked again at the boy's bicycle. And then I pulled away from the curb and drove on down Bay Street, unable to keep the grin off my face. Not even thoughts of a sick cow awaiting me at the end of my journey could stop me from smiling. I knew of only one person who owned such a poster, the biggest fan AđBA could ever have in the universe, a fan who knew every word of every song, who had found the big poster in a rare books and records store in Portland during our class trip to visit the Henry Wadsworth Longfellow house, and then had it framed for hanging and worshipping. I could still hear her voice, the day she found the poster, remember her pointing to each member of the band. "A∂BA is a letter for each of their names, Sammy," she said excitedly. "A is for Agnetha, B for Björn, B for Benny, and A for Anni-Frid." And so I teased her. "But one of the *B*'s is backwards. Is that supposed to be *cool* or something?" The more in love I fell, the more I teased. "What's a guy named *Benny* doing in a Swedish band?" I'd ask. "Shouldn't he be with the Bee Gees?" For whatever reasons, for whatever tricks fate had in mind, Dee Dee Michaud was moving home!

The farmer's cow, as I had suspected all along, was in need of some calcium, which is not untypical of milk cows. I hooked her up to an IV and let several liters of calcium run into her vein. When I was finished, I washed my hands in the farmer's kitchen, accepted a loaf of homemade bread from his wife, and promised Lydia would send them a bill. Then I piled back into my truck, tired but satisfied that my patient would soon be on the mend. On the drive home I couldn't stop myself from retracing my earlier route, even though I needed to gas up at Carroll's Sunoco, on the opposite end of town from Bay Street. The moving truck was gone, but a small green car sat in the drive, its back window piled high with items. The bike was now up on the porch, where numerous brown boxes had been stacked. On the front steps, a small boy sat staring out at the street, his chin in one hand. He looked about ten years old and, judging by the droop of his shoulders, he wasn't very pleased with his life at the present moment. *Poor kid,* I thought. *Moving to a new home is tough.* But I couldn't stop the truck, couldn't pull into the drive and say hello to Dee Dee's son. For one thing, I didn't know what I would say to his mother. It had been almost fifteen years since I'd seen her last, that night of our graduation, in June of 1982. I had made up my mind in the preceding weeks that I would tell her on graduation night how much I loved her, and I would finally ask her to go steady with me. I had practiced for days how I would slip my class ring— with its green Fort Kent High stone—off my finger and onto hers. I'd been ready to do just that until Dee Dee showed me the diamond that Bobby Langford had pushed onto that same delicate ring finger. What could I have been thinking? That's what I asked myself, as the years of my life stretched themselves out into more than a decade. Even after I met and fell in love with Lydia, I was plagued by these questions about my first attempt at romance. How had a quiet, shy young man such as me, with studious dreams for my future, ever believed that I could capture a carefree spirit like Dee Dee Michaud? She had been the kind of girl that lets life sweep her along in its stream. And I had been the kind of boy who stands on the bank, worrying about the strength of the current. But first loves die *very* hard. I was still haunted by those early images of her: Dee Dee dressed in camouflage clothing, snaking across a backyard on her belly in order to steal a dog because its owner kept it tied to a short chain. Dee Dee straddling the rail of the international bridge between Fort Kent and Canada, threatening, in French *and* English, to jump. Dee Dee crying her eyes out because Natalie Wood drowned alone in the dark waters off the coast of California. "Remember how she almost drowned in *Splendor in the Grass,* Sammy?" Dee Dee would sob. "When she knew she'd lost Warren Beatty forever?" Dee Dee Michaud had been born years too late. She had been a flower child, trying to survive in the onslaught of a "me" generation.

I sped on down Bay Street, away from the house at 204, and the sad boy lingering there on the front steps. What would Lydia think of me? A married man still carrying a high school torch that should have gone out years ago. I had other things to concentrate on, on that sweet May afternoon that had unfolded over Fort Kent, Maine, bringing with it the threat of evening showers. I had a clinic to run, and a house to build. Besides, when and if she was ready to reopen the past, Dee Dee Michaud would know right where to find me.

The stray puppy

THREE

If your heels be nimble and light,
You may get there by candle light . . .
—NURSERY RHYME

Fort Kent is a small place where big news travels fast. The very next morning Ross Cloutier called, his voice full of an excitement he was trying hard to contain. Ross supplied me with most news concerning people and issues from around the St. John Valley. He knew that I spent most of my time caught up in the workings of the clinic, or traversing the roads leading to the local farms. But I could tell that on this morning he was excited beyond the customary town news. He even dragged the conversation out, beginning with the weather, which was cloudy with a promise of rain.

"I kinda wish we hadn't gotten the traffic light," Ross said, and waited for my response. It was true that Fort Kent had just received its very first traffic

31

light, across from Quigley's Hardware on East Main Street. This would make things safer for the flow of traffic turning off East Main onto College, but talk around town had been divided on the issue. Some felt it was the best thing to happen to Fort Kent, while others ventured that perhaps Sodom and Gomorrah were doing just fine until *they* got *their* first traffic light. Finally, Ross got around to the real reason behind his phone call. I hated ruining this for him, but I couldn't help it, not after he'd gone to so much fine drama.

"Oh, by the way," Ross added, as if it were an afterthought. "Guess who's just moved back to town." I waited about three-fourths of a second.

"Dee Dee Michaud?" I wondered. Ross was quiet for a bit.

"How'd you know that?" he finally asked.

"It's on CNN," I told him.

"Damnit, Sam," Ross said. "You of all people shouldn't believe what you hear on television."

"It's either that or go downtown and watch the new traffic light turn," I said.

"Yeah, well," said Ross, not amused. "Just for the record, Dee Dee asked about you. We ought to get together. Like old times." Then he hung up without saying goodbye, a distinct *thud* in my ear. I had been teasing Ross Cloutier in this fashion since we played in Little League together in the second grade, and he'd yet to see one of my fastballs coming at him.

I thought about what Ross said. *We ought to get together. Like old times.* I wondered if that was possible. I had always put a lot of stock in what Mr. Thomas Wolfe said about going home again, that you actually *can't.* That's why I had never left long enough to feel that home was anywhere else but Fort Kent. I'd seen what time had done to the emotions of many townspeople who spent their adult lives working in some city, waiting for the day that they could retire and come back north, maybe build a little camp on the banks of the river. But for a lot of them the years had changed things too drastically and the place they had loved so only existed in their old memories and yellowing photographs. It was as if they were trying to put on an outdated suit, one that had shrunk in the dryer. They can look at it and know it's their suit all right, but it just doesn't fit anymore. Often, time shrinks childhood, too: that monstrous tree in the backyard isn't ninety feet high after all; that endless walk to Chamberlain's Grocery isn't ten miles, but a stone's throw; the mammoth field by Aroostook Car Sales where baseball games unfurled is now the size of a small driveway and filled with patches of crabgrass. What would coming back do for Dee Dee? Would she be able to make the transition? And now she had a son to worry about.

Two days went by and still no word from Dee Dee. I didn't take it personally. She would want to get a bit settled before she started seeking out her old friends. But on my way back from Eagle Lake, where I'd been examining a horse that was about to foal, I decided to swing out of my way and drive down Bay Street. There was the boy in the big backyard at 204, kicking at a football and looking as lonely as a boy in a strange town can be. I watched him disappear in my rearview mirror as I sped to the end of Bay.

At the clinic I went immediately to the back room and opened the cage where Lydia and I had put the black puppy—half Lab with a smattering of malamute. He'd been turned in just the week before, after Sherry Sullivan found him wandering about in the middle of Caribou Road, frightened, hungry, and about to be run down by a speeding car or truck. Sherry had knocked on every door for a half mile in either direction and no one seemed to own the dog, or even know where he'd come from. I suspected some dimwit had simply decided to get rid of him. I lifted the pup out of the cage and went out to the bulletin board that we keep in the front office. I took down the sign, *Stray Puppy to Good Home,* then I went back out to my truck, the puppy curled in my arms.

At 204 Bay I pulled up to the curb on the opposite side of the street. The boy was still there in the backyard. I lifted the puppy up off the seat and got out of the truck. I quietly crossed the street, doing my best not to be observed. I put the puppy down on the front lawn and then went back to my truck, where I could keep an eye on the dog. I waited to see what would happen. It didn't take long. As soon as the boy kicked his football one more time, the puppy shot off across the lawn in pursuit of it. The boy did what you'd expect a lonely boy to do when he sees a puppy: He scooped it up into his arms.

"Mom," he yelled. "Look what I found!" And then he disappeared through the back door of the house. Watching this unfold, I had to smile. Dee Dee had never turned down a stray animal, not once in all those years that I'd known her. The puppy would have a good home.

I was busily at work later that same afternoon when I heard the bell ring on the front door. I had just finished measuring out some pills for Larry Fitzherbert's cat—his wife, Judy, would be stopping by for them later in the day—so I quickly capped the container and went out to see what this latest client needed. It was Diana Catherine Michaud. Dee Dee. It had been almost fifteen years since we'd last stood face-to-face. What can I say? She was still beautiful, if a bit pale, but then she'd become a city slicker, and city slickers are usually pale. She'd lost weight, unlike the old Dee Dee, who was in constant battle with an elusive ten pounds. I couldn't speak, not at first. I must have looked pretty dumb, maybe even like some country hick, standing there with my

35

mouth open and a bottle of deworming pills in my hand. Funny, but I'd been expecting her. I knew in my bones that she'd drop by that very day. Yet she had still managed to catch me unawares and render me speechless, there in my own damn clinic.

"Sammy," she said. "How I've missed you." I wrapped my arms about her—it was like holding an old dream, something real and yet vague and glimmery at the same time. Time fell away. Time fell backward and the years disappeared as we stood there, my arms around her tiny frame. She had that same cool, fresh smell to her skin, not like perfume but something that speaks of the outdoors, the smell of a brook in the morning just as mist is rising up from the surface. I held her back at arm's length to look at her, the tiny brown beauty mark—she called it a mole—still etched above her upper lip, the blue-gray eyes, the perfect nose. Her hair was now shorter and darker, with blondish streaks laced through it—whatever it is that women do to lighten their hair. Dee Dee Michaud was home.

"I haven't seen you since graduation night," I said, when I was finally able to find words. "That was some pack of cigarettes you went out to fetch. Took you almost fifteen years." She smiled, her eyes turning even more gray there in the light of the clinic, small dimples appearing now. How had I forgotten the dimples?

"I hear you're the James Herriot of Fort Kent," she said. "Good for you, Sammy. I'm proud of you."

"Yeah, well," I said. "Don't believe everything Ross tells you." This pleased her. She'd heard the Sam Thibodeau–Ross Cloutier routine a million times before. "I'm glad you're home, Dee Dee," I added, "but you need to get some color in your face. Put on some weight." Before she could answer, the boy came bounding into the clinic, the black puppy in his arms.

"Lancelot just made friends with another dog," the boy said, as the puppy squirmed to be let down.

"I don't suppose you'd know anything about how this puppy got into my son's arms?" Dee Dee asked. I shook my head.

"Sorry," I said. "I'm a vet, not a cop. You want a cop, call Billy Caron. Did you know Billy became a state detective?" But Dee Dee wasn't going to let me change the subject.

"Then can you tell me how I might have this dog surgically *removed* from my son's arms?" she asked. Again, I shook my head. She smiled and motioned for the boy to step forward, and he did so, shyly. Dee Dee put her hands on his small shoulders. "This is my son," she told me. "This is Martin Samuel Langford, but you can call him Trooper." I smiled to hear this.

"Martin *Samuel,* is it?" I asked. Dee Dee nodded.

"I hope you don't mind," she said. Was she kidding? I was honored.

"Hey, Trooper," I said, holding out my hand for a shake. "How old are you?"

"Nine," he said. "Thanks for the puppy. Mom said it was you gave him to me."

"Tell you what," I offered. "I have a deal for all new residents of Fort Kent. Free neuters, free shots, and free heart pills for a year. Kind of like an animal Welcome Wagon."

"Sure you do." Dee Dee grinned at me. "That's how you stay in business." The boy gathered the puppy back up in his arms, now his very best friend.

"I named him Lancelot," he said, excited. Dee Dee tousled his hair.

"What a great name," I told him. "Lancelot was the bravest of all the Knights of the Round Table." The boy nodded in agreement.

"I don't think it was his *bravery* that attracted Guinevere," Dee Dee whispered. "I bet he had a great butt." Then she winked at me above Trooper's head. The same old Dee Dee. Older, maybe. Wiser, maybe. But the same.

"Welcome home," I said. I had never meant any nicety more than I did at that moment.

"So when am I going to meet your wife?" she asked, just as the clinic bell rang again and Alain Ouellette came in with his golden retriever, Swede, on a leash. The dog was limping.

38

"He cut his foot," Alain explained, as Dee Dee pulled Trooper and the excited puppy out of the way.

"Take him on back," I told Alain, and nodded to Room 2, the one with the examining table. I turned to Dee Dee. "Come to dinner," I said. "You and Trooper both. You can meet Lydia, and we can catch up on old times."

"You got a deal," Dee Dee said. "Let us know when." Then she rose up on her tiptoes and gave me a quick little kiss on the cheek. "Thanks, Sammy. For the dog. For everything. It's good to be home."

I watched as she and Trooper and Lancelot bounded down the front steps of the clinic and set off up the street toward Bay. I couldn't put my finger on what it was—looking back, I realize that I didn't even have a clue then—but I knew that something was missing in Dee Dee's eyes, that old fire that had never failed her before. It was something more than just time passing. But I couldn't dwell on it: I had to examine a golden retriever's padded foot.

Later that evening, as I drove home from vaccinating Mike Taggett's cows, I saw no harm in swinging past Bay Street, just to see how things looked now that the house was being lived in again. It glowed yellow and warm with inside light, while outside, statements were being made about the people who lived there: Trooper's bicycle, Dee Dee's little green car, potted marigolds, some seashell chimes dangling on the front porch. And, most interesting of all, an artsy wooden sign was now ensconced on Dee Dee's front lawn. I slowed to read the lettering in the gray dusk of evening: *Bay Street Candles,* the sign announced to the darkening world around it. I sped up the truck and beat it for home. It had been another long and exhausting day. And I now had a nip on the back of my right hand, the teeth marks of which could be traced to a certain golden retriever with stitches in his front foot.

Lydia was in our little upstairs parlor when I got home, reading, her glasses perched low on the bridge of her nose. I leaned down and gently kissed the top of her head.

"You're cute in those glasses," I told her. She looked up from her page and smiled at me.

"My contacts are soaking," she said. "Are you hungry?" I nodded.

We sat across from each other at the kitchen table while I ate a sandwich and some of the vegetable soup Lydia had made earlier in the day. I was as tired as I could be and still be functioning on my feet. But I tried to listen carefully as Lydia took a chair opposite me and then filled me in on her own day's experience as a small-town vet. She had had to put down a kitten that afternoon while I was out cruising the farms. Apparently, a dog had grabbed the helpless tabby up and shook it until its spine was broken.

Lydia was still upset. She had tears in her eyes as she detailed the event for me. I got up from my sandwich and soup—I was too tired to eat anyway—and came to where Lydia sat at the other end of the table, her knees pulled up to her chin. I put my arms around her and did my best to comfort her. For all of my life, I would remember the very first animal I'd ever put down, also a cat, back in vet school. As time goes on, and you find yourself more and more in that life-death situation with someone's pet, your senses dull themselves for what you have to do. But it never gets *easy*. They tell you at vet school that a good vet should stay as emotionally involved with the animals and clients as possible, but also be able to maintain a professional and objective distance. How do you do that? would someone please tell me. Just how the hell do you do that? It was far from Lydia's first time in that situation. But she was human.

"Come on," I said. "Let's get in bed and watch Letterman. He'll make us laugh." She smiled as she wiped her eyes.

"And how was *your* day?" she asked. "Anything unusual?" I thought about that. How had my day been? After I'd done my early morning stint in the clinic—and been nipped by Alain's golden retriever—I'd turned the clinic over to Lydia and gone out to inoculate those cows, check on a pregnant horse, drop off some medication. Same old, same old. And, oh yes, the very first love of my life had reappeared after nearly fifteen years. Anything unusual in my day, my wife wished to know.

"Not really," I said.

We were already in bed, in our pajamas, and Lydia was clicking over to David Letterman before I finished my answer to her question. "Oh yeah," I continued, as though the thought had just occurred to me. "An old friend of mine, my best buddy from childhood, has just moved back to town." Lydia stopped clicking and looked over at me, her face bluish and ghostly in the flickering light from the television set.

"Dee Dee Michaud?" she asked. I simply stared at her, the way I had stared at Dee Dee that very afternoon. I had never—not even during that early dating period when men and women foolishly tell each other *everything*—told Lydia about Dee Dee. I don't even know why, except that perhaps I was hoarding the memory to myself, protective of it.

"How did you know that?" I was finally able to ask.

"Ross," Lydia answered. "I saw him at the post office day before yesterday. He told me to be sure and ask you about Dee Dee Michaud, but I forgot." I smiled a facetious smile. Ross. The son of a bitch. Getting back at me for ruining his own news about Dee Dee. I just nodded.

"Well, she was my first friend," I said. I felt as though I was lying. But nothing had ever happened between Dee Dee and me. So why was I reacting in this way? I knew why. Because I had so badly *wanted* something to happen. "She and Ross and I had a lot of fun together." I waited. What else had Ross gone ahead and told Lydia about the past?

"Let's invite her to dinner," was how Lydia responded. Then she lay back to listen to Letterman's Top Ten List.

That night I slept better than I had in years. Funny, but just knowing that Dee Dee was there, a few streets away, back in her old house here in Fort Kent, made my life feel more complete, as if a piece of a puzzle had been missing for all these years but was suddenly found. It's like that in little towns. Everyone has known everyone else for so many generations that you grow, at the last of it, to seem like one big, diverse family. And Dee Dee Michaud, the prodigal daughter, was finally home, her dreams now curling above her head over on Bay Street, while off in the distance the sound of the bells ringing out midnight at the Catholic church, as they had for over fifty years, was loud and clear in the night air. The whine of a lonesome truck, as it shifted gears over on the Canadian side, grew fainter until it disappeared. A small breeze wafted in through the curtains, bringing with it the freshness of a new spring rain. I snuggled up close to Lydia's warm and sleeping body. Through the screen of the open window I could hear the first nighthawks of the season, winging around the yard light in search of insects. And just down the hill was the steady and constant murmur of the St. John, the childhood river where Dee Dee and I had searched under rocks for crayfish. Fort Kent was settling down for a peaceful night's sleep, so I closed my eyes and imagined that I was back in my old bedroom, my wall covered with Red Sox banners, a stack of *Playboy* magazines hidden beneath my bed. But this time, I had Lydia with me. I had both the past *and* the present, I told myself, as the web of sleep finally pulled me into its bosom. How could I go wrong?

Dee Dee's candles

FOUR

Tonight we sleep side by side,
like two new candles on a solid shelf...

And deep inside your womb
our firefly children dance.
—FROM *WIDOW'S WALK,* A COLLECTION OF POEMS

When Dee Dee and Trooper arrived for dinner on Wednesday night rain clouds had moved in over Fort Kent and a light shower followed them up the drive. I threw open the door and they hurried past, wet dark drops patterned on their backs. Dee Dee carried a colorfully wrapped box under her arm, Trooper a look of despair on his face: *a whole evening with grown-ups,* the look said.

"I wonder what Noah thought when he felt those first raindrops," said Dee Dee as she slipped her tennis shoes off and left them on the rug by the door, a gesture neither Lydia nor I required of our guests. "I mean, did he know it was the Big One?" Trooper smiled against his own better judgment about adults. But I could see right away that he already held his mom in better esteem than he did most people over eighteen years old.

"It would have been a good time to open the first umbrella shop," I said. Then, my voice imitating that of a zealous TV announcer: "What does she have in the box, Don Pardo?" I gestured to the gift under Dee Dee's arm. This time, Trooper actually smiled. There was hope for the evening.

"It's for Lydia," said Dee Dee as she and Trooper followed me into the parlor. Lydia was still at work in the kitchen, chopping green pepper for the salad.

"Lydia," I called out as I poured Dee Dee a glass of wine. "They're here, and they've come bearing gifts." Lydia appeared in the doorway to the little parlor, a dish towel in her hands and a smile on her face.

"Good," she said, "that's the best kind of visitor." And she reached a hand out to Dee Dee.

I had been thinking about this moment all day, that second in time when Dee Dee and Lydia would meet, the very two women who were in orbit around my life. It wasn't that I expected a full-fledged catfight, but I had decided nonetheless to be careful. I didn't want Lydia to feel jealousy, so the last thing I needed was for her to catch me staring at Dee Dee like some lovesick high school kid. But the truth of the situation was that—while the man in me was happily married to Lydia—the high school kid still *did* have that blasted crush on Dee Dee Michaud. Unrequited love is the worst kind. It can leave you feeling like that one sock left behind in the clothes dryer. But I was certain that after Dee Dee had been back in my life for a while, I would finally come to terms with that night back in 1982, our graduation night, the night I was going to ask her to go steady. Things would settle, like river silt, and our lives would eventually get back to normal. All I had to do was to hide my infatuation with Dee Dee from my wife.

What happened next threw me for a loop. Dee Dee handed the wrapped box to Lydia, who took it and eagerly opened it up. Inside were two long, tapered white candles.

"I made them," Dee Dee said as Lydia lifted the candles from the soft tissue they'd been carefully wrapped in.

"They're lovely," she exclaimed, and I could tell she meant it, which was fine, but usually Lydia doesn't run with the Martha Stewart crowd. She'd prefer to be in old boots, tramping about the woods for wild mushrooms, rather than coming up with a brilliant and innovative way to fold the dinner napkins. Yet here she was, gushing over Dee Dee's homemade candles.

"You really made them yourself?" Lydia was asking as Dee Dee nodded proudly. She ran a finger down the length of one taper.

"I'll show you how sometime," said Dee Dee. "It's not difficult."

"That'd be great," said Lydia. "You're so talented."

"Well, look at you," Dee Dee countered. "I hear from the gossip vine that you're an excellent veterinarian."

"Thanks," Lydia said. "Come on. Let's put the candles on the dinner table."

They left the room in a swirl of gushing and oohing and aahing. So much for the big catfight. Good thing I hadn't sold any tickets. I glanced down at Trooper. He was staring at them, too, his dark eyebrows pushed upward, as if questioning. I felt an instant sadness for the two of us. It was true: Sometimes we men just don't have a clue.

"Want a soda pop?" I finally said to Trooper. "Orange juice?" He looked up at me, an *it's just us guys* look on his face.

"Sure," he said, as if sensing that this would placate me.

"Come and eat, gentlemen," Lydia called from the dining room, and Trooper and I were both rescued from a moment of male awkwardness.

We ushered ourselves into the tiny room, where Lydia was searching for matches and Dee Dee was pulling back a chair for Trooper. He climbed into it and thumped his elbows onto the table as Dee Dee sat down across from him. I went back out to the kitchen and looked up on the shelf over the stove for a book of matches—*Thibodeau's Insurance Company*, the cover read. This was one of the town's oldest businesses, founded by a distant relative of mine, but I had always seen an irony in their matchbook ads. After all, we were insured by Thibodeau's, so how would it look if our house burned down because of *their* matches? I gave the book to Lydia, who quickly struck a match on the outside flint strip and then carefully lit the two tapered candles. The wicks caught the flame quickly and burst to life.

"Every time you light a candle," Dee Dee said, watching them flicker, "an angel is born." Trooper shook his head.

"Ah, Mom," he said. "Not that angel stuff again."

"What a lovely thought," Lydia said to Dee Dee. "I can't say I believe in angels, but it's a sweet sentiment." Trooper shot me another male look. I was going to get along just fine with Trooper, I could tell. We were cut from the same cloth, even if it wasn't silk. Maybe, after dinner, while Lydia and Dee Dee discussed angels and candles, he and I could catch the last inning of the Red Sox game.

We took our places around the table as Lydia served her special casserole, eggplant parmigiana, one of the few dishes she'd learned to make. By now, all of our friends in Fort Kent had eaten it several times. Ross referred to it as "eggplant á la Lydia." The wine might keep changing at our dinner parties, but the main course rarely wavered: it was usually purple.

"So, Dee Dee," my wife said, "Sam tells me you

51

had a crafts shop in Wyoming." She passed Dee Dee her quota of eggplant—at least for that evening—and Dee Dee took the plate and put it in front of Trooper. She waited for the second serving. It was easy to see that Trooper came first in her life.

"It was just a small shop," she said, "a little corner store that sold homemade odds and ends. Mostly items crafted by the locals. And, of course, candles. That's where I learned to make them. I even gave candle-making lessons, you know, to make ends meet."

"I saw your sign," I told her, afraid that if I didn't speak the two women would fail to remember that I was there, that I was alive, that I was the one who had brought them together on this rainy evening. "Bay Street Candles. It has a nice ring to it."

"Candle making is my biggest passion," Dee Dee went on. "There's not a lot of money in it, I'll admit, but there's certainly lots of enjoyment."

"Why don't you offer lessons here, in Fort Kent?" asked Lydia. Dee Dee considered this.

"Do you think a class would fly here?" she wondered. Lydia was not to be hampered in her enthusiasm. Maybe she *would* like to spend an afternoon folding napkins in a creative way, maybe she'd been pining for just such an opportunity. Trooper ate his eggplant. He had long ceased to shoot me little apologetic glances. I was on my own, Trooper had decided.

"Oh, I bet it would fly like the wind!" Lydia assured her. "I'll certainly take it." Well, there you have it. You think you know someone. You think you know your own wife. It was a good thing we weren't on *The Newlywed Game* right then. We'd have a big fat zero as our score, for all America to see.

"Then maybe I *will* offer classes," said Dee Dee. In the candlelight, her pale skin held a beautiful golden sheen as light flickered on her high cheekbones. The blondish streaks scattered among the brown of her hair seemed to catch on fire with highlights. *Don't stare,* I warned myself the second I became aware that I'd been gazing at her as though she were some kind of rare painting. *For God's sake, don't gawk.* I looked at Lydia. She was too caught up with the candle-making class to have even noticed.

"We can put an announcement here at the clinic," Lydia was saying, "to let people know about the class. Then there's the bulletin board at Paradis Shop & Save. And you can put a notice in the *St. John Valley Times.*" Blah. Blah. Blah. Yak. Yak. Trooper reached for a second slice of bread, probably just for something to do. Sympathetically I passed him the butter.

"Then it's settled," said Dee Dee, giving me an approving look. "I'll be teaching a class in candle making, and I've already got my first student." She and Lydia held up their glasses of wine and toasted each other. May I never live to see another catfight so spiteful and vicious. I nudged Trooper's elbow.

"Want to catch the last of the Red Sox game?" I asked, and his face lit up as though he had eaten the entire book of matches from Thibodeau's Insurance.

"After dessert, okay?" Lydia asked and I nodded. Sure, why not. What was wrong with another few minutes of the Mutual Admiration Society that had unfolded before me at the table. Damn her. Damn Lydia. Wasn't she just a tad threatened? After all, Dee Dee was beautiful, passionate, intelligent, and let's not forget *single*. I was beginning to feel like that one sock again, but with lots of lint stuck to the heel.

"So how'd you get the nickname Trooper?" I asked the boy. Otherwise, I feared he might fall asleep. He shrugged his small shoulders.

"Mom gave it to me," he said. Dee Dee heard this, and broke off her conversation with Lydia, something about how Louise's Magic Mirror was a good place to get one's hair cut.

"Because you have to be a *trooper* in life to be good at it," Dee Dee said. She winked at Trooper. I stood up and motioned to the boy.

"Come on, Trooper," I said. "I'll show you the clinic and then we can catch the last of the game." Trooper bounded up, as if he'd been waiting for some cosmic cue, some heavenly recess bell.

Downstairs we visited the animals first, in the backroom cages, two dogs and three cats. In the

54

morning I'd do three neuters, two spays, and two teeth cleanings. The cats and dogs broke into a chorus of yaps and meows as we entered the room, the cats springing to the bars of their cages, where they made rapid figure eights in a desperate plea to be petted. Trooper obliged by offering a comforting finger through the bars, stroking the fur of each animal when he could reach it. The clinic itself held an instant fascination for him, the shelves of bottles, the surgery table, the X-ray view box, the anesthesia unit, the cautery unit, the scales, my big microscope. I let him handle the stethoscope, and the rubber plexor I used for checking reflexes. He carefully inspected the ophthalmoscope. Then he stood back to survey the surroundings, impressed with the needles, syringes, the bottles of injectables, the various solutions and ointments. Every vet clinic keeps a cat or two on the premises as potential blood donors for when a situation demands a quick supply. Some clinics keep in-house dogs as well. Our clinic cats, Ralph and Simon, former strays, were now large and sleek and spoiled. Trooper smiled to see them lounging on the windowsill by the back door.

"This place is neat," he said, and I smiled. It *was* neat. Ever since I'd been a little kid I'd wanted to grow up and become a vet, to save animals. It had only taken four long years of college, with a heavy concentration in biology and chemistry, and then four long years of veterinary school, after which I emerged with a fifty-thousand-dollar student loan. But I'd done it. I'd become a doctor of veterinary medicine. I looked around again, seeing the clinic through Trooper's eyes this time, and I felt a warm surge of pride. It was definitely a *neat* place.

It was almost nine o'clock and Trooper was starting to doze beside me on the sofa when Dee Dee and Lydia came upstairs from Lydia's workshop. Lydia had been showing her the leaf press that she kept there, a device for preserving and studying the various foliage in the area. Lydia had also developed an interest in the rare plants that grew along the St. John riverbank, especially the Furbish lousewort, named for Louise Furbish and thought for years to be extinct until it was discovered growing only in the St. John Valley.

"Hey," Dee Dee said, when she finally broke away from the conversation on flora long enough to notice that we were still alive. "Did you guys have a nice visit?" Trooper stood and stretched his arms.

"Guys don't *visit,* Mom," he said, matter-of-factly.

"That's right," I said, coming to his defense. "We might vegetate once in a while, side by side, but we certainly don't *visit."* Dee Dee smiled. She laced her tennis shoes back up and motioned for Trooper to put on his own shoes.

"We gotta go, Troop," Dee Dee said. "Lancelot must be lonesome for us."

"Sam?" Lydia said. "You'll drive Dee Dee and Trooper home, won't you?" I stood and imitated Trooper by stretching my own arms and legs. The game against Baltimore had been about as interesting as candle making.

"Sure," I said. Why not. The two royal princesses were done chatting. Time for the mice to turn into footmen and escort one of them home. "I'd be happy to," I added. The truth was that I was genuinely anxious to get Dee Dee to myself. Lydia had dominated her attentions all night long. Funny, but I was afraid Lydia would feel jealousy, and yet I was the one to do so. Dee Dee shook her head.

"Let's walk, Sammy," she said. "Like the old days. Remember how we used to dream of having our driver's licenses one day so we wouldn't have to walk?" I nodded, and took my jacket off the coatrack. Trooper bounded down the steps ahead of us and out the door to where his bicycle waited. On the front porch Lydia said good night to Dee Dee, and the two hugged a soft embrace, with promises of seeing each other soon. Then Dee Dee and I were off, down the summery night streets of Fort Kent, on our way home to Bay Street.

"Remember that blue bike I bought with potato-picking money?" Dee Dee asked, as we watched Trooper cutting circles on his bike on the empty street in front of us. I remembered. She had sold it to Jimmy Desjardins, the day she felt too grown-up to

57

be riding on a bicycle anymore. She must have been about thirteen. I remembered that time well because she'd also started developing that same summer, small hills beneath her blouse that somehow managed to grow into mountains each night in my dreams.

"I'd give anything to have that bike back," Dee Dee said. "What good exercise it would be. I wish I had it to give Trooper. You know, an antique from my past."

A sweet spring evening fell in about us as we walked on, a fresh smell of wild cherry on the breeze. When we reached Main Street, we turned west and walked down past the old JCPenney store, Laverdiere's Drug, Nadeau's House of Furniture. Martin's Pharmacy was no longer there, and Dee Dee made mention of this as we passed by. It was now a Radio Shack, but at Martin's we had twirled on the red leather stools that lined the small soda fountain on one end of the store. We'd eaten egg salad sandwiches and drunk Cokes and waited for the years to pull us out of sleepy adolescence. Martin's Pharmacy was now gone, but in its place were CDs, televisions, and stereos waiting to be given a home. "Remember Warren Harvey?" I asked Dee Dee, and she nodded. "Well, he owns Radio Shack now," I told her. As we walked on, Dee Dee grew quiet. Just before we reached Bay Street she looked up at me, sadly.

"Trooper never knew his dad," she said. I kept my eyes on the boy riding the bicycle ahead of us. "He was less than a year old when Bobby went chasing some dream to Alaska. He doesn't keep in touch with us anymore. I don't think he ever really wanted a kid." I put my arm around her shoulder, to offer what comfort I could.

"But *you* sure do," I said. "Anyone can see that. All it takes is one good parent." She nodded, and we walked on, slowly, our feet recognizing the sidewalks of the town we both knew so well.

"You aren't going to say *I told you so* about Bobby Langford?" Dee Dee wanted to know. I shook my head.

"Not just yet," I said. "I'm waiting for the perfect moment." She nudged me in the side, just below my ribs. Dee Dee's nudge. I wondered how many of them I'd received in my years of being her friend.

"I want Trooper to grow up in this town," Dee Dee said as we passed Country Cottage, its window full of books and gift ideas. She had grown serious again. "Just like I did. In Fort Kent he'll always have people who care about him, if anything should happen to me."

We stopped in front of 206 Bay and stood staring at the house that I had known as *home* for most of my life. The family that bought it were busily living in it. Inside shadows fell upon the curtains and then disappeared as people moved from room to room.

People living their lives. As my family had once lived a part of our own lives, behind those windows, beyond those doors. Another family now.

"It's a strange feeling to no longer have you next door," Dee Dee said, her eyes on the front window of my old house. "For the past few nights I've been waking up, unable to sleep. I've been getting out of bed and going to my window, so that I can look over at *your* old window, just like I used to do when we were kids, and I was afraid of the dark. I always felt such comfort that you were close by, Sammy. Some nights, I could almost hear you breathing as you slept." I nodded. I knew what she meant. I'd been there. Done that.

"Listen," I said. We had walked up onto the porch at 204 and stood there, waiting for Trooper to pull his bike up the porch steps. "I could use a helper at the clinic, just light chores, cleaning the cages, feeding and walking the animals, that sort of thing. If Trooper is interested. Say, three days a week, after school? The money's not great, but it'll support a nasty comic book habit." Dee Dee liked the idea instantly.

"Hey, Troop," she said. "Sam needs a helper at the clinic, taking care of the animals and all. You interested in a job?" With his right foot, Trooper slapped the kickstand down on his bike and leaned it on its side. Then he came to peer up at me, his brown eyes intent.

"You mean it, Sam?" he asked.

"Sure," I said, "if you're up to it." He beamed as I held out my hand and we shook. "Can you start this week?" He looked at Dee Dee for an answer, and she nodded approval.

"Neat!" said Trooper, and then he raced inside to find Lancelot. Dee Dee turned to me.

"Thanks, Sam," she said. "He really does need a male role model in his life." Well, she didn't have to convince me of that, not after our earlier experience at dinner. I looked down at Dee Dee just then, her blue-gray eyes so determined, a fierce protection shining in them for her son. But there seemed to be a sadness there, too, and this worried me. What demons had followed her to Fort Kent? Demons no doubt brought into the world by Bobby Langford.

"You can always tell me if something is wrong," I said to her. She nodded.

"Just like old times, huh?" she asked. I leaned down then and kissed her lightly on the cheek, her skin soft and silky.

"It's so good to be home, Sammy," she whispered, and I felt her small arms wrap themselves about me for a good-night hug.

As I walked home, I glanced over at the lights twinkling on the Canadian side, and wondered if I meant the kiss in the friendly way that Dee Dee had accepted it. I could still feel that old surge of passion for her. Who wouldn't? How can you get close to

61

someone so alive and not catch the fever from them? Not want to wrap yourself up in their zest for life? Dee Dee still had this effect on me, on the people around her, as Lydia herself could now attest to.

That night Lydia and I made love for the first time in weeks. It seemed that our different schedules at the clinic, our frantic jousting in the small-town rat race, kept us too tired to think of anything beyond Letterman's monologue. But not on this night, a night that had begun with eggplant casserole, and homemade candles, and a flickering old flame flown back into my life like a fragile moth. A magical night.

Afterward, Lydia lay with her head on my chest and listened as I told her about hiring Trooper as our helper at the clinic. She liked the idea instantly.

"He's a lonely boy," she said. "It'll be good for him. And for you, too." I wasn't sure what she meant by that last remark. After a few minutes passed, minutes in which I let my thoughts roam to the mystery of just what it was that had brought Dee Dee Michaud home, I was certain that Lydia was asleep, her head there on my chest. I listened to the occasional traffic at the end of the street, teenagers on their way down to the Irving station for a soft drink, most likely. Beer if they could find someone to buy it for them. Dee Dee and I had done that often enough in our prime. But after a time, Lydia spoke, a small voice rising out of the night.

"You know, Sammy," she said, "it's okay that you still love Dee Dee a little." I looked down at her, her face mottled with light coming in from the street, and I was thankful for the semidarkness. Thankful that she couldn't see my face, my eyes. I was never good at lying.

"What are you talking about?" I asked. Lydia laughed.

"I'm talking about the crush you have on Dee Dee," she said. I was shocked, and I told her so.

"Whatever makes you think such a thing?" I wanted to know. This amused her further. She lifted her head and looked squarely at me. I could finally make out her eyes, there on her face, dark ovals before me.

"You're kidding, right?" Lydia asked. I shook my head. I was feeling as embarrassed as a teenager caught with his hands beneath the bedsheets. But this time, by my *wife*, instead of my *mom*.

"Dee Dee is my childhood friend," I said. "She and Ross both."

"All I'm saying is that it's all right that you've still got a crush on her," said Lydia. "I think it's just natural. After all, I still have a crush on Freddy Stolinski."

"I do *not* have a crush on Dee Dee Michaud," I insisted. I could feel my face and neck burning just a bit and was thankful again for the cover of darkness. I kicked my toes up under the blanket, loosening it from its tight tuck. I hated a tight tuck.

"I think it's sweet," said Lydia. "That's all."

"There's nothing for you to think sweet," I said again, this time with a bit too much anger. I knew Lydia was waiting for this sign: anger in me meant she had hit the nail on the head. "Damn blanket!" I added, and kicked at it again with my feet. Lydia giggled triumphantly, then turned her back to me. With a quick jerk she pulled her share of the cover over to her side. I said nothing for a long time. We lay side by side, Lydia's steady breathing keeping up a sweet rhythm next to me in the dark. I watched the passing trail of car lights race across the ceiling—cars headed home from the late movie showing at the theater on Hall Street. When I was certain that Lydia had fallen into the first comfortable stages of sleep I flicked my toes against her bare leg under the cover.

"Hey," I said. "Hey, you. Wake up." Lydia groaned as she pushed toward consciousness.

"What?" she finally mumbled.

"Who the hell is Freddy Stolinski?" I asked.

The colt and the mare

FIVE

How far that little candle throws his beams!
So shines a good deed in a naughty world.
—WILLIAM SHAKESPEARE

Trooper proved to be a fine little worker. Added to this was the fact that he genuinely loved the animals at the clinic. I had made a good choice in hiring him. And Dee Dee was right: He needed a father figure in his life. The way I saw it, it would work two ways. Troop would get a surrogate dad, and I would get some experience at playing parent, for the day when Lydia and I would have our own kids. I was wondering how different girls would be from boys, and whether nature would give us the opportunity to find out, when the phone rang. It was Clarence Freebaker, whose farm sat about five miles from town in a clutch of poplar trees. Clarence Freebaker, owner of the pregnant mare. His voice was full of contained excitement and I could tell he was doing his best not to panic. From what I could make out, the mare was having a tough time foaling.

"I'm afraid I'm gonna lose her, Sam," he said. I told him not to worry, that I'd be there by the time he hung the phone up, poured himself a shot of whiskey, tossed it down, and then walked back out to the barn. This seemed to calm him. He thanked me and hung up.

Trooper was straightening the shelves in the back room and I quickly yelled to him. This would be a good time for the boy to witness some of what my job entailed, especially since he'd been telling me from his first day at work that he wanted to be a vet, too. I could only hope that his mother didn't think he was too young to share in nature's biggest display of magic, the wizardry of birth. But I had to believe that someone like Dee Dee wouldn't tell a child that babies came from cabbage patches, or by the good graces of the stork. Besides, all farm kids know from an early age about birth. And Trooper was turning into a regular farm kid. He loved tagging along in the pickup as I made my rounds of the neighboring farms. I had only to yell once before he was right on my heels as I dashed to the pickup and pointed it toward the Freebaker farm.

Standing in the barn door, Clarence greeted us with a grim face. I moved past him and followed his pointed finger. The mare was lying on her side, contracting. Usually, all a vet has to do when a horse gives birth is to stand there and watch. But in this case, the mare had been straining, trying hard to push the foal out, yet it wasn't moving down the birth canal. She would need an assisted delivery. That meant that I would have to mildly sedate her. Since I already knew this horse, knew her to be gentle, I decided to give her a half cc of detomidine, injected into her right or left jugular vein, both easy to locate. She was lying on her left side, so I chose the right vein.

"This is known as the *jugular groove*," I said to Trooper, and traced with my finger the area running from the angle of the mare's jaw to the base of her neck. Trooper listened intently as he stood with my medical bag near his feet, waiting to reach down and assist in any way he could.

"It'll take effect in about five or ten minutes," I told him, and he nodded, his eyes round with excitement. This would make the situation less dangerous for the mare *and* for me. Once the sedation kicked in, she'd stop straining while I assisted in the birthing.

With Trooper peering over my shoulder, I rolled up my sleeves and did a vaginal examination. I needed to be sure that the foal was in a normal position in the womb. I was relieved to feel that it was just as it should be, lying on its chest with its forelegs extended forward.

"It's in a good position," I told Trooper, and

Clarence, who was now bending over Trooper's head to watch. "Imagine someone diving into a pool," I added, when I saw his quizzical look. "Both forelegs are extended forward, one a little less extended than the other, with the chin resting on the knees." I demonstrated by putting my own arms into a diving stance. Trooper nodded, understanding. "Now, if the neck was flexed to either side instead of pointed straight ahead, we'd be in big trouble. It's the one kind of delivery that's simply impossible." But the neck was flexed straight ahead. Clarence's foal would be fine.

Just as I'd expected, it wasn't long before the tiny hooves appeared and I saw that their bottoms faced downward, toward the feet of the mother. Perfect. All that was necessary now was to apply some gentle traction on the foal's front legs, in sync with the mare's own pushing. I motioned for Trooper to pass the OB chains, and he quickly did. Contrary to the image that *chains* might call forth in our minds, these stainless-steel chains are not at all traumatic to the foal. I let Trooper help as I secured the chains around each of the foal's front legs, just above the fetlock. It was time to pull, and pull hard. A foal should always be delivered in twenty or twenty-five minutes, whether the mare is getting assistance or not. But with the added help of the chains, and along with the mare's natural pushing, the process is usually over in five or ten minutes.

"Like this," I told Trooper, and he took one of the chains in his small hands and pulled, just as he saw me doing. His mouth was open slightly, and I could hear his rapid and excited breathing as the foal's chestnut-colored knees appeared, then the soft wet muzzle, followed by the head, which was emblazoned with a beautiful white diamond. And then the shoulders appeared—the most difficult part of any delivery, considering their width—and finally the trunk of the foal, hips, and hind limbs. It was over. Clarence Freebaker's foal had entered into its new world as it existed in northern Maine, a world made up of a nicely fenced twenty-acre pasture, a fairly new barn with a dazzling red roof, a cool blue creek running through the wooded back acres where it could wade in the hotter summer months, a surplus of oats, and plenty of hay grown last season on Clarence's own back forty. The foal came into its safe and self-contained world, a rush of amniotic fluid spilling out behind it.

A cool breeze filtered in through the wide barn doors, and that's when I felt a stream of sweat inching its way down from my forehead and onto the side of my face. I wiped it away with my shirtsleeve, looked over at Trooper, and smiled. No matter how many times I'd witnessed it in the past—dozens and dozens of times, bad births, good births, you name it—it still always caught me unawares, staggered my imagination, trapped my breath in my throat for a few seconds. Here before me was a mixture of genetic coding, a tiny formula that had been put in place months earlier, and now, thanks to that single DNA message, I was looking at a perfect, miniature horse, ready to stand in a few minutes and take on a brand-new world.

"We need to let the mother and baby rest for a while," I said to Trooper. I could see that the foal, a male, had started breathing normally. "It needs a little time to get its bearings," I added. I looked up and saw that Clarence Freebaker was now leaning back against the wall, watching from a short distance, a look of relief spilled across his face. Clarence had always been of the mind-set that nature equips an animal with what it needs to carry on the natural processes. Veterinarians were an unnecessary expense. At least he thought that until an incident occurred during my first year of practice, an incident that changed his mind forever. It was 2 A.M. when my ringing phone jarred me out of a nice warm sleep and set me on the dark, rainy road to the Freebaker farm. Clarence had a mare that was having trouble foaling then, too. And he'd decided to let nature run its course, rather than phone a vet. He called too late, however, and while we saved the mare that night, we lost the foal. It's almost impossible to correct a foal's position within the uterus. In extreme cases an epidural is given to the mare, but if the foal isn't born within thirty minutes after labor begins, it's almost always born dead, due to a lack of oxygen. A C-section can be performed, of course, but that usually requires an equine surgical facility. It's just not a good idea to perform a C-section in the field. The odds of a mare surviving are slim. So Clarence lost his foal that night. Now he saw a lesson in it all, I suppose. From then on he kept a close eye whenever one of his horses was about to give birth. "If it looks as if anything's the matter," Clarence had said, "I'll give you a call first thing." It was the best way he could tell me he'd been wrong, that nature sometimes needs a push herself.

As we waited, the mare slowly rose to her feet, breaking the umbilical cord in the process, and passing the placenta. Now the little foal was really on its own. But the mother would be nearby for some time yet. She had already begun a methodical licking of her newborn baby, nuzzling it gently. I saw Trooper's eyes widen.

"Wait till Mom hears about this," he said. "What next, Sam?"

"We need to give the baby a physical exam," I answered, "to make sure all the parts are working well." He smiled at this. "We'll start at the nose and finish with the tail," I added, as I opened the tiny mouth and saw that the palate appeared normal.

"Making sure it wasn't born with a cleft palate," I answered Trooper's wondering look. Then I shone a penlight into the wide eyes and saw that they reacted normally to the light. I listened to the heart. It sounded fine. No murmur. The umbilicus also seemed normal, not leaking any urine. I disinfected it with a simple tincture of iodine solution, one that vets have been using for many years. Then I finished off the rest of the exam, checking for any hernias, seeing that the genitalia appeared normal, and that all reflexes seemed in order.

"He's as perfect as a baby horse can be," I told Trooper, who grinned with pleasure to hear this. "We'll wait to make sure it stands and nurses," I added. "If that doesn't happen within an hour, it means we've got some trouble on our hands." Ordinarily, since everything looked fine, I would've let nature and the mother horse handle things from here on out. I did have two neuters to perform that afternoon, along with a spay. But I wanted Trooper to see the foal actually stand.

Clarence's wife turned up with a pitcher of lemonade and some cups. But Trooper didn't want any. Instead, he sat with legs folded under him on the barn's floor, and kept his eyes riveted on the baby horse. Every now and then he'd look up at me and ask, "How long has it been, Sam?" Finally, that same genetic coding, that amazing message from the brain, told the little horse that it was time to try those new legs. He had been lying quietly, pressed next to his mother, for almost fifteen minutes, so it was time. As we watched, the colt tried again and again to get the spindly legs to work. But again and again the legs flailed and he went back down into a small chestnut heap. Finally, after fifteen minutes of failure, success! The colt stood on wobbly legs that bent in and out like tender reeds in a strong wind.

"Wow," said Trooper. It was the best word I could think of myself. What an amazing thing to be born damn near running! Now the colt began to nurse, pushing its soft muzzle against its mother's stomach until it made connection. I picked up the empty syringe and threw it into Clarence's trash can in the corner and then collected my bag. Clarence reached out a hand to shake.

"You send me the bill," he said. "You're worth every penny," he added as Trooper and I walked back to the truck. I had to smile. That was as close as Clarence Freebaker could come to telling me he'd made a mistake that rainy night a few years earlier. It was as close as he could come, and it was plenty good enough for me. Most farmers are men of a few words. I simply nodded.

"You'll get a bill all right," I told him. Clarence took off his hat, wiped his forehead with his shirtsleeve, and stood looking out across his lower pasture, already dotted with yellow splashes, the first buttercups of the season. Soon the field would be a blanket of red and orange hawkweed, with thousands of fireflies flitting about, and summer would be swift upon us.

"We're gonna get some rain," Clarence Freebaker noted, bobbing his chin up at the sky. End of the conversation about horses. I got the hint as I, too, stood and studied the firmament, doing my usual bonding with Clarence before I could feel it was okay to pile into my truck and whip back down the road. Sure enough. The cumulus clouds, those puffy fair-weather clouds that I'd noticed earlier in the day, had piled up into cauliflower shapes and were no doubt on their way to becoming cumulonimbus: thunderheads. Clarence might not know such Latin words as *nimbus* and *cirrus,* but he knew, after a lifetime of studying the signs, that rain was headed toward his farm. I nodded in agreement.

"We can use the rain," I said. And then Trooper and I were free to sail down the stretch of gravel road leading back to town.

On the drive home, Trooper asked some questions I'd expected: *What happens if the foal doesn't come out right? Had I ever seen one born dead? Does it hurt the mother horse?* Typical stuff.

"Where is the father horse?" he suddenly asked. I had to think about this one, because it threw me for a loop. Was the father horse sunning itself on a farm in the South of France? Taking in the waters at some corral overlooking Montego Bay?

"Well," I said, choosing the words carefully—this was Dee Dee's job, after all. "I suspect it's one of those male horses Mr. Freebaker has there in his pasture. You know what? I think it might be worth-while to swing by the new McDonald's and get us each a vanilla milk shake. As means of a celebration. What do you say?" Trooper seemed to like the idea all right, but before I had time to reach the end of the road leading out to Clarence's farm and turn back to-ward town, he was deep in his thoughts, his shoul-der resting firmly against the door, his eyes tracing row after row of newly planted potato field.

"You thinking about how that milk shake should come with a large fry?" I asked, and gave him a play-ful poke on his arm. He looked up, almost surprised to discover that he was sitting in the pickup truck, there on the seat beside me. He shrugged. After a few more minutes of morose silence, he turned to look over at me.

"Sam?" he asked. "Did you know my dad?" I tried not to show any expression at all on my face, other than concern for my driving.

"I didn't know him well," I replied. "Just for that year he moved up to Fort Kent, and met your mom. The year before I graduated from high school."

"Did he make friends?" Trooper asked. "Moving to a new place is tough. You gotta leave all your friends behind." I smiled at him as I thought about his question. Did Bobby Langford make friends? How could I say: *Sure, Troop, he made friends with everybody who desperately wanted to buy some pot from him.*

"He had lots of friends," I said, "but he was older. He was in high school. I think it's tougher to move to a new place in the early grades." Trooper nodded, and seemed thankful that I understood this deep, dark tenet of life: *It's tougher in the early grades*. This seemed to warm his mood. Now he wanted to talk.

"What was my dad like, Sam?" he asked. I prayed for the McDonald's arches to hurry up and loom into sight. I was dreading just such a conversation between Trooper and me, and I had intended to ask Dee Dee what I should do, what lines I should learn, for when it did happen. But I'd put it off, like I'd put off filing my income tax and so had to ask for an extension. I'd simply stuck it on that back burner of good intentions, with all those other pots, and now reality was descending upon me like a damn red-shouldered hawk.

"What was he like?" I repeated, killing a few more seconds of time. "Well, let's see. He was very popular. A good basketball player. And he had one of those personalities that made people want to be around him a lot. He was a cool guy. Like Fonzie." Trooper listened somberly, nodding at each of my declarations. He liked what he heard, especially the Fonzie remark. And it wasn't as if I was lying to him. Bobby Langford, with his James Dean good looks, was as popular as they came—that's how he'd managed to snag Dee Dee Michaud in the first place—and probably would have been popular even if he wasn't selling weed on the streets of Fort Kent. And a couple of times I *really had* seen him shooting a few hoops with the boys at the high school basketball court. He had a good, sure aim and could dribble as though narcotics agents were right at his heels. "And he was very good-looking," I said, "just like you are." *Come on, McDonald's. Come on, McDonald's. Come on, McDonald's,* I thought as Fort Kent's only traffic light finally blinked green and I was free to turn right and head for that milk shake. But Trooper was not to be pacified with ice cream and milk, not after the new experience he'd just undergone in Clarence Freebaker's barn, the experience of *parent and offspring.*

"Mom says he was a dreamer," Trooper continued, more to himself than to me. "She says he took off to Alaska like a leprechaun looking for a pot of gold. Mom says don't blame him, you can't expect more than that from a dreamer." I smiled. It would be so like Dee Dee to give Trooper the truth by wrapping it in some nice, poetic gauze.

"Dreams are different for all of us, Troop," I said. "Mine was to become a vet and settle down right here in Fort Kent, Maine. It wasn't a daring dream, not like wanting to climb Mount Everest or run the Amazon River in a canoe. But it was still a *dream.*" The first of the yellow arches loomed into sight and looked as beautiful to me as that star in the east must have looked to the Three Wise Men.

"Still," Trooper said as I pulled into one of the few

parking slots, "some dreams can be pretty stupid." I looked at him for a few seconds, feeling helpless as I groped for words, feeling just like that newborn colt that had struggled so hard to stand on its new legs.

"What would you think about an apple turnover for dessert?" I finally asked.

The international bridge

SIX

Night's candles are burned out,
and jocund day stands tiptoe
on the misty mountaintops . . .
—WILLIAM SHAKESPEARE

I have a poster hanging in my office at the clinic, a sou-venir from my four long, hard years at Boston's School of Veterinary Medicine. It's on the back side of my office door, where the public can't see it. But it pretty much sums up, philosophically, an aspect of veterinary medicine that goes unnoticed in the minds of many of my well-meaning clients.

Why I Want to Be a Veterinarian

1. To gain decorative scars about the hands, arms, and face.
2. So I can get paid half as much as an MD for twice the work.

3. Because you can always muzzle vicious animals, but people . . .
4. I didn't. I thought this was law school.
5. Because formaldehyde makes me feel sexy.
6. Because I'm masochistic. I like eight-day weeks.
7. Because it's a zoo out there.
8. For the tremendous cultural respect showered upon veterinarians.
9. Because I can express anal glands better than I can express my own opinion.
10. So I can listen to people ask me "Why didn't you become a *real* doctor?" for the rest of my life.

Mostly, I try to be understanding when my clients commit any of the above sins, but I have to admit that even after all these years that last one can still get my dander up faster than all the other nine combined. And often it comes from people who should really know better, such as the occasional nurse. But one particular thorn in my professional side is Jerry Peterson, from my old science class back at Fort Kent High School. Jerry went off to become a gynecologist and, like some of us, found himself right back at the source. He'd opened his own practice in Fort Kent and had set about curing gynecological ills and delivering his share of Fort Kenters into the world.

But every damn time Jerry made an appointment to bring his cat or dog into the clinic, I found myself gritting my teeth. Lydia would often sneak behind my back and call Jerry, making up some excuse as to why his appointment needed to be changed and that he would now be bringing his pet to *her*. Lydia knew from experience that it would be days before I'd come down from a Jerry Peterson visit, days of banging bottles in cabinets, of tossing prescriptions onto the desk in the outer office, and, most important, days of snapping at my innocent and loving wife without even realizing it.

So, on this *Thank-God-It's-Friday* Friday, it would be to Lydia's horror when she learned that Jerry, probably tired of constantly having his appointments rescheduled, dropped by the clinic, impromptu as hell, with his cat tucked under his arm. It had been a long, hard day and I took a deep breath in anticipation of the fact that it was just about to get harder. The cat had come down with a simple upper respiratory infection, a URI, or so it seemed after I took its temperature and auscultated its lungs. The lungs and the heart sounded fine, so I gave it an injection of amoxicillin and dispensed a seven-day follow-up supply. Jerry studied the prescription label on the bottle as though it were the Rosetta Stone.

"Amazing," he said. "That's exactly what a *real* doctor would prescribe."

When Lydia returned she knew right away that

there had been some kind of derailment of my emotions while she was gone. She put a handful of letters down on the desk, along with a brown bag from the liquor store that held a bottle of sake for the Chinese food I'd promised to cook for our dinner. Then she came around to the back of my chair and started kneading my neck muscles with her fingers. It felt good, but it was hardly a sufficient antidote for my anger.

"May I ask you something?" Lydia finally spoke. I nodded. "By any chance, did Jerry Peterson stop by here while I was gone?" I tossed my pen onto the desk and it bounced over the edge and disappeared.

"Egotistical and vain little bastard," I said. Lydia's fingers dug deeper. "What makes you ask?"

"Just a wild guess," she answered. Then she swiveled my chair around so that she could look at me.

"You call Ross. I'll call Dee Dee and Trooper," she said. "Let's go to the seven o'clock movie. It's just what the doctor ordered." I considered this.

"A *real* doctor?" I asked. Lydia frowned.

"Oh my," she said. "So Jerry *has* been by."

Lydia and I walked to 204 Bay Street to gather up Dee Dee and Trooper, who had both agreed that a spur-of-the-moment movie might be just the thing to end a long day. As we approached Dee Dee's house, Lydia spotted Lisa Ornstein, the folklorist and director of the Acadian Archives at the campus, walking down the other side of the street. Lisa and her husband, Nick Hawes, were also outstanding and well-schooled musicians, and Lydia had her heart set on violin lessons. In the hopes that Lisa might have suggestions about where to find an instructor, Lydia darted across the street to catch her. I went on up Dee Dee's front steps. The door was cracked open, and since they knew we'd be coming to fetch them, I assumed it was an invitation to come on in. So I did.

No one was in the front parlor, but I heard voices filtering out from the back room where Dee Dee did most of her *candling,* or whatever it's called. Sure enough, Trooper and Dee Dee were busy in the back room. Dee Dee was hovering over a double boiler of what must have been paraffin wax, and it appeared that she was teaching the boy how to make his own candles. Poor Trooper, but that's just what he was being: a *trooper.* I stood in the doorway, waiting for an opportunity to get a word in, to announce to them that I was there, but Dee Dee was on a roll.

"Remember, Troop," Dee Dee was telling him. "Every time you light a candle, an angel is born. That flicker you see is the very first breath an angel takes." Trooper sighed.

"It's just a candle, Mom," he said. I felt a

sympathetic sneer form on my face. *Attaboy, Troop,* I told myself. But Dee Dee's enthusiasm was not to be quelled by her son's disinterest.

"It isn't *just a candle,*" she protested. "Candles have to be made carefully, by applying layer after layer, in the same way that a person grows, year after year. Anytime you're ever sad and lonely, all you have to do is light a candle, and then sit back for five minutes and watch it burn. That's not too much to ask of yourself, is it? Just keep your eyes on that candle's breath, and before you know it, whatever was bothering you won't seem quite so bad. Can you promise me you'll do that?" Another big, and certainly understandable, sigh from Trooper.

"I promise," he said. Dee Dee leaned down to kiss the top of his head.

"Good," she told him. "That way, if anything should ever happen to me, you'll always feel me there with you, especially during those times when you'll miss me." I had been just about to break in, until Dee Dee made that remark; the moment had turned suddenly personal between mother and son, and now I felt as if I'd been eavesdropping on a private conversation. I tiptoed back to the front door just in time to see Lydia crest the top step out on the porch. Good. It would appear that we were just arriving, together.

"I think they're in the kitchen," I told Lydia, as I slammed the door behind us.

. . .

Within minutes Dee Dee, Trooper, Lydia, and I were strolling down Bay Street, on our way to Hall Street, where we would meet Ross in front of the movie theater. Ross had divorced over a year earlier, a sad time for him and even for us, his friends who cared about him. His ex-wife, Amy, had moved down to Portland with their only son, Randy. But Randy, at ten years old, had not been able to adjust well to a new school. He missed his dad, and he missed Fort Kent. So Amy had agreed to let the boy come back north and live with his father. She would drive up once a month to visit him, and Ross would take the boy to Portland once a month. They would do what they could to help Randy through a tough period of adjustment. And now that Ross seemed to be serious over Vickie Perreault, his coteacher, Randy would have a good female role model around.

Ross had told me that Randy was back, but I hadn't seen the boy yet. Now, there he was, standing in front of the movie theater with his dad, and looking every bit a potential best friend for Trooper. I wondered why I hadn't thought of that before as I introduced the two of them. As we stood chatting for a few minutes, the boys drifted off into a conversation of their own. They seemed to hit it off right away, and now they were anxious to get inside the theater so that they could see the advertisements for upcoming movies.

"You know," said Lydia, "I'm not really up to a movie. I just wanted to get Sam out of the house so that he wouldn't drive me crazy. Our famous Dr. Peterson stopped by the clinic today with his cat. Need I say more?"

"Pretentious little jerk," I snarled.

"Egotistical prick," Ross muttered, softly, so the boys wouldn't hear him. I nodded. I appreciated the support.

"I don't feel like a movie, either," said Dee Dee. "I just needed to get out of the house, too. Seems I haven't gone out in ages."

"Me, too," said Vickie.

"How about we go to Bee Jay's and read the ceiling?" Ross asked, and four heads nodded happily. It was exactly what we all needed. A cold pitcher of beer and a few bowls of salted peanuts at Bee Jay's, where oil paintings done by some of the local craftsmen and craftswomen adorn the walls. There are a couple of pool tables, too, and cribbage boards, and the ceiling is covered with large advertising tiles, mostly business pronouncements from the valley's sons and daughters. It was the best idea possible for that balmy spring-turning-into-summer night. And since the two boys had hit it off so well, they could sit through the movie together.

"After the movie," Ross was saying to Randy, as he shoveled him out a fiver, "you can go to

McDonald's for a bite. Trooper's your guest, okay?" The boys couldn't have been happier to get rid of the adults. They disappeared into the theater in a burst of energy. They'd be fine. Not only were they responsible boys, but Fort Kent was a safe place for children. And we all hoped it stayed that way.

A few cars were parading up and down through town, folks coming in and out of stores as we walked. It's easy to spot a neighbor or friend on the streets of Fort Kent, Maine. *Everybody* doesn't know *everybody* in town, but pretty damn close.

"I can't believe the JCPenney store is gone," Dee Dee said as we walked. It was true. The old building—which ceased to be a store and became a bar, the Lone Star, shortly after my generation was old enough to shop—had burned to the ground two years earlier. Nobody ever figured out how a bar in northern Maine came to be known as the Lone Star in the first place, what with painted cacti and bronco riders decorating the walls. We just assumed it had been another case of wishful thinking, this time on the part of the first owner during a particularly long winter. But now it was gone, and with it one of the oldest buildings in Fort Kent, the kind that have the towering false fronts, architecture that implies the building is really taller than it is.

"But at least the Fort Kent Hotel is still here," Dee Dee added. And so it was, sitting just across the street and still doing a brisk bar business. Having been built at the turn of the century, the hotel represented the older, more historical aspect of town.

We passed the China Garden, and then Sirois' Restaurant, before we crossed the street to Bee Jay's Tavern. Then we paused for a moment, looking across at Clair, Canada, where the streetlights had just begun to sparkle in the encroaching dusk. Folks from Fort Kent and Clair often darted back and forth across the border, living with a foot in both countries most of the time. Lydia and I occasionally stopped by the bowling alley in Clair for a relaxing game of candlepin. Afterward, we often dropped in for Chinese food at the Maple Leaf restaurant. "I know it's Canada but why do they call a Chinese restaurant the Maple Leaf?" Lydia had asked. I had an answer for that one: It had been just a little Canadian restaurant at its inception. The bamboo shoots and the fried rice and the fortune cookies had come later.

We stood looking at the big green international bridge that spanned the St. John River between the two countries. We watched as Ann Gendreau came out of her booth at the American customshouse, wearing her customs uniform. She waved a warm hello to us, and then leaned over to talk to the driver of the car that had just pulled up for clearance. Dee Dee shook her head.

"Some things just never change," she said. "It

seems like I've been looking over at Canada all my life."

"Well," I said. "Canada's still there, looking back at us, and we're still here. We were just waiting for you to come home." She seemed to like this, but it stirred up a different idea in Ross Cloutier's mind, old hippie that he was.

"Hey," he said. "I been thinking. We should start our band up again. This town is more ready for the Acute Angles than ever. Oldies but Goodies are hot." Dee Dee and I smiled. It would be so like Ross to think of such a thing. Half his brain was trapped in the sixties, even though he'd been a kid when that decade had exploded upon the American social scene.

"I'll be your manager," Vickie offered.

"And I'll be your only groupie," Lydia added.

"No way in hell," I said, and Dee Dee nodded, agreeing quickly. But Ross was fired up. He motioned for Dee Dee and me to come closer.

"Don McLean's 'American Pie,'" Ross said. "From the chorus." Like the fools that we obviously still were, we stood outside Bee Jay's, near the big wooden tub of flowers, and sang in harmony while Vickie and Lydia pretended not to know us. It's one thing to sing about good old boys, and Chevy cars, and drinking up a river of booze. But the last line of the chorus, the one about dying, sent a chill through me. As we finished, no one said a word. We just stood there as a quick and sober silence descended over us. I remember it to this day. It was as if a soft shower of rain had passed over our heads—ours and no one else's—as we stood there in the evening air in front of Bee Jay's.

"Let's go get a beer," Dee Dee said, breaking the spell. "I left town before I was old enough to drink at Bee Jay's. Lise always caught me and threw me out. It's gonna feel great to sit at a table and be legal."

"I hope you brought your ID," Ross said as he held the front door open for the rest of us. "Lise is still pretty strict."

Bee Jay's has been around ever since I can remember, the only place in town where you can have a drink in front of a roaring fireplace in the heart of winter. Some of us appreciate that. And we like looking at the oil paintings on the walls, some done by friends and acquaintances, for sale to tourists. Sue Roy, for instance, likes to paint local nature scenes. A moose knee-deep in some lake, with mist rising up toward the dawn. Those paintings kind of make Bee Jay's part bar, part museum. And the ceiling tiles make it part advertising company and genealogical chart. Along with the Fort Kent Hotel, Bee Jay's figures pretty high in the social lives of some of us, a meeting place of sorts where we can visit with folks we might never see otherwise. But the place wouldn't be the same if Lise Boucher wasn't there. A pretty French-Canadian woman now living on our side of the border, Lise started working at Bee Jay's in 1972 and now most of us looked for her smile when we came stomping in.

"A pitcher," Ross told Lise, "unless you're now serving beer in *barrels.*" Lise gave us the smile and then went off behind the bar.

"She's still got her French accent," Dee Dee whispered. "That's nice."

The jukebox was playing, as it seems to perpetually at Bee Jay's. The pitcher came and then the stories started to fly, all prefaced with *Remember when we did this?* and *Remember when we did that?* Dee Dee seemed enchanted by this; after all, she was home where she belonged. And Lydia was having a fine time, getting what she called the "female" version of some of the war stories she'd been told by Ross and me. Somehow, we didn't come off as brave and witty in Dee Dee's version of the same event.

"My favorite memory of all?" Dee Dee asked, suddenly pensive. "The Winter Carnival when we went to Quebec City. Remember how we pooled our money so we could stay at the Château Frontenac?" Ross and I nodded in sync. It had been a splendid time for eight of us, all packed on the floor of one room in sleeping bags, unbeknownst to the managers of the hotel. And we had drunk French wine and watched the sun rise over the St. Lawrence River. A terrific time. Our ancestors had come up that very river almost four hundred years earlier. We were connected by a long and sturdy thread to the history outside that window. And, young and drunk as we were, we had all felt it instinctively.

"It's at moments like that, you kind of think you'll live forever," Dee Dee said, and we nodded solemnly. And then someone played Sheryl Crow on the jukebox, "Leaving Las Vegas," and the dark mood lifted like a great bird and flew away. Talk now focused on the tiles on the ceiling, each one a two-by-three-foot business card replica for some local company. Or for former locals who now lived and owned businesses elsewhere: Gagnon Electrical Service, Bristol, Connecticut; Cyr's Auto Body Shop, Waterville, Maine; Belanger's Dress Shop, Quincy, Mass. All people with a past in Fort Kent, Maine. All people connected. All you had to do to get on the Ceiling of Fame was pay the thirty-five bucks and an old tile would be taken down, a new one would be painted with your own declaration, and *voilà!* You would hang from the ceiling, as if from the roof of heaven. Ross had secretly commissioned one for the veterinary clinic, shortly after Lydia and I moved to Fort Kent and opened our doors. Then he and Amy had invited us down to the tavern for a beer, had situated us directly below the large tile, and after we'd had a couple brews, they'd simply pointed upward. Lydia and I were official, *Northern Maine*

Veterinary Clinic now imprinted on the ceiling. Ross pointed our tile out to Dee Dee and she giggled with glee. I looked up, smiling with pleasure. Ross had managed to get the tile in a great spot, right in front of the fireplace and directly above the large table where we liked to sit. Next to it was a commemorative tile for a summer writing workshop depicting a large tombstone, with the names of all the students engraved on it, and a special thanks to the teacher, a Ms. Pelletier. On the other side was a business ad for Bouchard's Chain Saw Sales, which had been there so long that it was dark and faded. But the brightest tile of all was Northern Maine Veterinary Clinic, Sam Thibodeau, DVM, & Lydia Newhart, DVM. Let others say it was foolish to feel pride. But I have the heart of a small-town guy, and this is my town.

"Good thing there aren't any prostitutes in town," Ross was saying now as he nodded at the ceiling ads. The others laughed hugely at this. But something descended over me again, and this time it was like a great, black chill. Lise was back, asking if we wanted another pitcher, and I heard Dee Dee decline. We had to go get the boys, she told Lise. I was there with my best friends, with the past curled neatly about our table and chairs, with the past curled like Jerry Peterson's cat at our feet, and yet I was observing my friends from a distance. It was like being in a car wreck, when everything slows down so that you can pay close attention to the fate that awaits you up ahead, in the crash and the busted glass. And there I was, at the wheel. I looked around the table at the cheerful faces of my friends, faces alive with the moment, alive to the sound of the old jukebox blaring away in the background. It was now playing "The French Song," a traditional song hundreds of years old, but such a favorite among Franco-Americans that you could find an old record on most local jukeboxes, a song we had heard played at all the St. John Valley weddings over the years of our growing up, a part of our heritage: *Quand le soleil dit bonjour aux montagnes, et que la nuit rencontre le jour. Now when the sun says hello to the mountains, and the night says hello to the dawn.* But instead of feeling blissful, with a few glasses of beer in my belly to speed the bliss along, I was overcome with a sadness I couldn't explain. I stared at Dee Dee's beautiful face, the wide eyes still sparkling, and I felt an unnatural fear settle down on me. *Je suis seul avec mes rêves sur la montagne. Une voix me rappelle de toi. I'm alone with my dreams on the hilltop. I can still hear your voice though you're gone.*

When we left the bar, I was still dazed. It was a spectacular night, with spring slowly drifting like a cloud toward summer. I could only hope that the walk might clear my head.

At McDonald's the boys were ready. Ross

mentioned homework to Randy, and Dee Dee said that she and Trooper would need to work on his spelling for an hour before bed.

"He spells like I do," Dee Dee whispered.

"I'm exhausted," I heard Lydia say. "There are times when it's not so bad to be parentless, and this is one of them." Overhead, the constellations were sparkling, not enough light pollution to obscure them. As we walked, I listened to hear Dee Dee pointing out the brightest stars for Trooper, then identifying the constellations they were found in.

"The stars will always be there for you, Troop," she told him. "Stars are candles, too. Candles of the night." Trooper had just been to see the science-fiction movie *Men in Black,* with Tommy Lee Jones and Will Smith battling weird and comic aliens. He was not buying any of this, especially in front of his new friend.

"Ah, Mom, stars are stars," he said, matter-of-factly, just as we reached our street. And then Lydia and I separated from the others. Their piece of the world broke away from ours, and I watched as my dear friends, my old comrades from childhood, grew smaller and smaller, disappearing as they strolled down the street.

"Are you okay, Sammy?" I heard Lydia ask. "You seem kind of spaced-out. Too much beer?" I nodded that it was, indeed, a glass of beer too many, although I'd had only three. I could still hear Trooper and Dee Dee, their voices trailing away in the distance, still arguing over the Star and Candle Theory. Lydia and I linked arms and walked home, a regular thirties-something couple out for a stroll. I tried to imagine us walking that same street, arms linked exactly as they are now, when we were in our seventies, children scattered like seeds on the wind, grandchildren breathing somewhere on the planet: Lydia and I, approaching the last days, the apex of our lives. It saddened me immensely, those thoughts about our mortality. While I didn't endorse an afterlife, I was still struck occasionally with how unfair the whole idea is: We live to die. I had always tried to guide and shape my life by a simple philosophy: If it won't matter in fifty years, then it shouldn't matter now. I thought of Dee Dee's words earlier, words spoken to her young son. *If anything should ever happen to me, you'll always feel me there with you, especially during those times when you'll miss me.* Those words had been turning over in my mind all evening long, biting at me, nagging.

"You've been working too hard," I heard Lydia say. The voices of my friends were now gone, vanished, their footfalls faded, no longer able to be heard, their laughing faces evaporated into thin air. They seemed suddenly, and utterly, lost to me.

"I need a hot bath," I said to Lydia. I was instantly cold, a chill running through my bones. Only the

100

warm light, shining out from our little hard-earned clinic as we turned up the street toward home, could spark an ember of safety in me once more. But even that seemed a fleeting and ghostlike thing, just another gossamer piece of the American dream.

Dee Dee's window

SEVEN

'Tis not necessary to light a candle to the sun.
—ALGERNON SIDNEY (1622–83)

Our lives progressed onward with the slow, methodical certainty that comes from living in a small, safe town. I kept busy with springtime births and vaccinations on the surrounding farms, while Lydia held down the clinic. Our lives continued onward in much the same way but for one exception: Lydia had signed up for Dee Dee's candle-making class, and now our kitchen table was covered with newly bought paraphernalia. The most engrossing conversations I had with my wife nowadays usually began with me asking, "What the hell's *that* for?" But Lydia seemed genuinely excited, and as long as the class made her happy, gave her an opportunity to get out and meet new faces, I didn't care a whit. But I wasn't prepared for the mysticism that seemed to evolve around the notion of melted and cooled paraffin wax.

On the first night of the class, I stood in our bedroom door and watched Lydia sweep her long brown hair back into its usual tie. Then she brushed a bit of powder across her nose, made a couple sweeps across her lips with a tube of reddish lipstick.

"Are there any good-looking men taking this class¿" I asked her. Lydia was rarely interested in makeup. Her natural good looks was one of the first things that had attracted me to her. Like most men, I prefer women without red nails long enough to rip flesh from bone, or lips buried in an ocean of color, or eyes that have been swamped with the latest fashionable shades, lashes gobbed in mascara. But every now and then Lydia liked to dab a little red to her lips, a little powder to her nose. I never knew when these sporadic moods would come upon her, or what might have caused them. I had only questioned her once about it. "It breaks the monotony," had been her reply, and it was good enough for me. Now, as I watched her getting ready, she seemed almost like a schoolgirl, going off on her first day of class. But Dee Dee could always bring out the child in the people around her.

"Dee Dee's got this philosophy," Lydia said as she selected a green sweater from her drawer. "It's so corny, it's cute. Look at the instructions that come with a box of her candles." She nodded at a rose-colored cardboard box lying on the bed. I lifted the top to find beneath rose-colored tissue two hand-made candles, still attached by their mutual wick, and a folded piece of parchment paper. The words were scrawled in a purple ink, in Dee Dee's own hand:

" 'Dear candle owner,'" I read aloud. I looked over at Lydia. "Don't tell me you need a *manual* to own a candle?" I asked. She frowned.

"Don't be funny, Sammy," she said, hoisting the green sweater over her head. I have always thought that there is such sheer poetry in seeing a woman slip into a blouse or sweater, her arms raised, her throat thrust backward. It always reminded me of that poem by Robert Frost, about how birches that have been bent low from an ice storm look like women with their hair trailing over their heads. Pure poetry. Maybe I'd missed my calling, after all. Maybe I should have been a poet. I'd have to discuss this with Trooper later.

"Will you quit staring at me like you're some kind of serial killer?" Lydia asked. "Just read the note." All right. Okay. So I'd been staring transfixed at my wife, the woman I loved, the woman with whom I intended to have children. So shoot me. I went back to the note.

Dear candle owner. Each candle is magical. Each candle has a life of its own. When you feel

105

loneliness and sorrow, when you feel deep dark anger, light a candle. Then sit quietly for a few minutes and watch it burn. You will be transformed, for each candle is your guardian angel.

"Jesus," I said. "This is too New Age for me."

"I know," Lydia agreed, "but I think Fort Kent is ready for a bit of candle magic. Dee Dee puts quotes on the back of each box, too. Sometimes they come from poems and novels. Sometimes they come from song lyrics. But each quote has the word *candle* in it. Cute, huh?" I nodded sarcastically and then turned the box over. Sure enough, there was the quote for the day: *When the moon shone, we did not see the candle.* And then, beneath this: *William Shakespeare (1564–1623).* I looked over at Lydia, who was now in jeans and lacing up her tennis shoes.

"Lyddie," I said. "This is starting to sound like Moonie stuff. I'm not going to have to hire one of those specialists to kidnap you, am I? To take you away from those candle classes for deprogramming?" Lydia grabbed the box from my hands and stretched up on her toes to give me a quick kiss.

"You might," she said. I wrapped my arms around her. It felt good just to hold her. Our busy days at the clinic had kept us too often apart, running full speed in opposite directions. I nuzzled her neck.

"Know what my mom always said?" I asked.

"What?"

"Choose neither a woman nor linen by candle-light," I quoted. "It's an old sixteenth-century proverb." Lydia pushed me away, a wry smile on her face.

"For one thing, it *belongs* in the sixteenth century," she said. "And for another, I don't believe your mother *ever* said that. You and Troop have a good night." And then she was gone, off to Fort Kent's very first class on the artistry of candle making.

It was usually right after school each Wednesday that Trooper cleaned the cages in the back and filled all the food and water dishes. But he had asked me earlier in the week if he could do it on this night instead. I saw no problem with that. After he finished with the last cage he came into my office, where I was doing paperwork, and asked in his inimitable way if we could have a man-to-man. This meant that he sulked on a chair until I could finally get him to tell me what was on his mind. That's how I found out that it was no accident he'd chosen the night of the candle class to coincide with his cage-cleaning chores. So we decided that he could rotate his schedule permanently, if it was okay with his mother. He would never, ever—at least not if we two men had any power over it—have to meet up face-to-face with any candle-making afficionada.

When he finished his chores, Trooper asked if he could go upstairs and watch television until Lydia came home, an indication that the path was free for him to go home himself. I told him to grab some of the spaghetti left over from dinner while he was up there, and went back to my paperwork. I needed to order supplies and it seemed the forms I was filling out were endless.

In no time at all Lydia was back, her arms full of even more junk, and a glow of candlelight in her eyes. She'd had a great time, she told me, as I sat there thinking about how good she looked in that green sweater, and imagining all that Robert Frost hair flailing over her arms as she took it off. I looked at the clock. It was still only nine o'clock. I could leave the rest of the paperwork until morning. I even remembered a fairly decent bottle of wine in our little wine rack upstairs. A bubble bath, I decided, would sound very romantic to Lydia, and yes, damnit, *candles*. She could even burn what she'd made that very night, unless they were designated for the Smithsonian. But it was not to be.

"Where's Trooper?" she asked, suddenly serious. I told her that most likely he'd fallen asleep in front of the television set, since I hadn't heard from him in almost an hour. Lydia's face was suddenly lined with concern, and so I stood up, pushed my chair back, and closed the office door.

"What's up?" I asked. So much for a good bottle of wine and a romantic evening with my wife.

"It's Dee Dee," she said. "I'm worried about her,

Sam. She seems, I don't know, *fragile*. She just doesn't look well. I think she's let herself get run down." I listened, but I had to suppose that being a single parent was a tough job, and raising a boy without a father there to shoulder some of the burden was even tougher. Dee Dee always had energy to spare, but she tended to use it all up. "Take Trooper home," Lydia added. "See what you think. If you agree with me, then maybe you can talk to her." I considered this. My wife—who seemed as sexy and inviting to me right at that moment as she ever had, who was *the very reason* I'd been thinking about green sweaters being slipped off, and jeans unzipped, and corks popping out of bottles of wine all evening—my *wife* was sending me *in this condition* to check up on the other sexy, provocative, luscious, alluring woman in my life, my first love. *And an unrequited one at that!* Talk about sending a match on a mission through Gasoline Valley. A firecracker into the inferno.

"Okay," I said, and looked around for my jacket. Then I muttered, "But don't say I didn't warn you."

"What did you say?" asked Lydia.

"Nothing," I replied, and went upstairs to wake Trooper.

Trooper was too sleepy to talk on the short drive over to Bay Street. That was fine with me. Guys can do that. They can sit side by side at a dock and fish

109

for hours without much more than an occasional grunt or nod to each other. And guys can go on long trips in automobiles and never say more than a dozen words. I tried to imagine the candle class taking place with a surfeit of words. Wouldn't happen. We have some differences, men and women do, and that just happens to be one of them. And I'm sure nature has her reasons for this, maybe because women are nurturers and part of nurturing is placating. I knew what Lydia would say: And men are just overgrown babies who *need* nurturing. Well, now I was being sent on a mission as nurturer, and on a night when my testosterone level was higher than it had been back in high school.

From the street I saw that Dee Dee's front room, the old parlor, was aglow with candles. Danny Nicholas was just pulling away from the curb, his wife, Naomi, on the passenger side. Naomi, who worked at the university as the president's secretary, must also be taking the candle-making classes. Two more women, obviously the last of the Candle Cabal, were just leaving. Trooper raised himself up in the front seat and peered intently at the figures lingering on the porch.

"That's Mrs. Chevalier," he said glumly. "She kisses me and gets my face all wet. And she pinches my cheek." I nodded. I knew how the kid felt. Mrs. Chevalier still did that to *me,* every time she brought her damn Pekinese into the clinic. I shut the headlights off and pulled the truck into the yard, all the way up to the little garage in back. I turned the engine off and rolled my window down so that we could hear the voices on the front porch. And Troop and I sat there like a couple of gargoyles waiting calmly in the shadows of evening, our cheeks dry and unpinched, at least for that moment in time. Finally, good-nights were said all around, and Mrs. Chevalier and her costudent were off. Dee Dee came to the edge of the porch and leaned over the railing to peer at us.

"What are you two lunatics waiting for?" she asked.

"Coast must be clear," I said to Trooper. "Let's go."

Dee Dee took Trooper upstairs and instructed him to run a bath before bedtime. At least *someone* would get to soak in hot water and bubbles. I even considered going up to recite "Birches" for Trooper as he splashed around in the tub, but then Dee Dee shouted down to me, asking if I had time for a glass of wine. I felt like poor Faustus, poor son of a bitch, about to make some pact with the devil from which there would be no return. I was nothing but thankful that Dee Dee was wearing an apron similar to the one worn by my own sweet, saintly mother. And she had some god-awful, thick-soled shoes on her feet, the kind nurses wear as they rush about hospitals and sickrooms. I was thankful for the apron, but

I was ecstatic to see the shoes: It's the tall, spiky-heeled kind that drive wise men to do foolish acts. I shouted back up the stairs that a glass of wine would be fine. Then I went into the parlor and waited for her. While I did, I silently made more vows of chastity than any serious monk ever made in the course of a long monkish life. I made more vows than Leonard Cohen, out in his California monastery. *Just remember Lydia's face,* I kept telling myself. *Or Remember the Alamo. Whatever it takes.*

But I needn't have worried, because Lydia was right. Dee Dee didn't look well. Her face was far too pale, and beneath her eyes were dark half-moons. Either she was run down and overworked or something was seriously wrong.

"Dee Dee," I said as she passed me a glass of wine. "You look tired. Even Lyddie noticed it tonight. Are you feeling okay? Maybe you should see a doctor." Dee Dee just smiled at me, that wicked little smile she always kept for times when she felt I was being too big-brotherly.

"This has just been a difficult time," she said. "For Trooper and for me, what with the move from Wyoming and all." She poured herself a glass of wine, took off the apron, which she obviously wore when pouring paraffin side by side with Mrs. Chevalier, and sat cross-legged before me. She looked suddenly like an innocent little girl, and I felt instant guilt for any previous carnal thoughts.

"Tell me something, Sam," Dee Dee said. She took a sip of wine and I followed suit. "You ever wonder how your life would have turned out if you'd made different choices?" She ran a couple of fingers through her hair, and waited. The truth was I didn't believe in that sort of thing. It was like trying to play a poker hand by imagining what you would have bet if you'd gotten *four* aces, instead of *three*, two pairs of *kings* instead of two pairs of *deuces*. It's a pretty useless exercise, and I told Dee Dee so. What I didn't tell her is that, while I don't replay the cards life has personally dealt to *me*, I often replay the cards it's dealt to *others*. Did I ever wonder what might have happened to Dee Dee Michaud if she hadn't run off at the age of eighteen and married the wild and good-looking Bobby Langford? You bet I did. Until I met Trooper, that is. That boy, who was starting to feel as close to me as my right arm, was reason enough to justify a foolish mistake made in the passion of youth. After those days of having Trooper in the clinic, or bouncing around on the pickup seat next to me, I had come to feel a certain respect for Bobby Langford. That same genetic coding that had so amazed me every time I saw an animal being born was also present in Trooper. And half of it had been inherited from Bobby. I had come to feel a kind of pity for Bobby, that his own foolish and youthful mistakes had kept him from knowing this fine boy.

"No," I said to Dee Dee. "I never wonder about

what might have been, because it's useless. Energy wasted. I only wonder about the things I can still change." Dee Dee seemed to like that answer. She raised her wineglass, as if to toast me.

"Me, too," she said. "At least, I don't wonder anymore, not after I had Trooper." I smiled. She'd just hit the nail on the head. Trooper made all those mistakes worthwhile. Just don't make them again.

"Here's to your kid," I said, and toasted her back. I still couldn't get over how shallow her face had become in such a short time. *Fragile,* that was Lydia's word, and it kept coming back at me. I waited for her to respond, but she seemed to be thinking deeply about other things, maybe other lives we might all have lived. The candles kept up their steady flickering as they danced across her face. We heard the sounds of boys arguing on the street out front—the way we used to argue, over baseballs, and candy bars, and bottles of Pepsi. Suddenly, Dee Dee looked up at me, catching me quite off guard.

"Sam?" she asked. "If anything ever happens to me, would you and Lydia take care of Trooper?" I was shocked to hear this.

"What would make you ask that?" I wanted to know. "You're sounding very fatalistic and that's not like you." Dee Dee shrugged.

"When you're a parent, you'll understand," she said. "It's just a matter of safeguarding your kid." I supposed this must be true.

"Of course we'd take care of Trooper," I said. "But nothing is going to happen to you, so don't talk that way." Dee Dee just smiled.

"Sometimes I worry," she told me, swirling the wine in her glass. It had turned to pure burgundy in the candlelight. "I don't have any living relatives, Sam. That means Trooper would be alone." I nodded.

"Well, worry no more," I said. "Lydia and I would never turn our backs on Trooper. Do you have any idea how difficult it is to get good child labor these days?" Dee Dee's face lit up, all happy again, her eyes peering at me from a distant place. "But you've got to promise me that you'll see a doctor," I added. "Will you do that?" Dee Dee nodded. She would do that.

It was not quite ten o'clock when I got back home. I took off my shirt as I climbed the stairs to our apartment, remembering Lydia in the green sweater, green as a field of shamrocks. She wasn't in the living room, so I threw my shirt on the sofa and headed for the bathroom. I imagined her waiting for me in a tub of hot water, a glass of wine at the ready, some soft music on the radio. I poked my head around the door and stared at a waterless tub. Empty. I took my pants off, flung them over the curtain rod, and tiptoed to the bedroom. I would jump onto the bed and catch her off guard as she waited

115

for me beneath the covers, probably in that slinky rose-colored negligee that she got out every once in a blue moon to turn me on. I swung around the corner, prepared to leap. There was Lydia, as sound asleep as Goldilocks could ever hope to be. She was lying on top of the covers and wearing an old pair of cotton pajamas. *My* old pair of cotton pajamas. So much for the rose-colored negligee. I eased her body over and pulled the blankets from beneath her. Then, I got her into bed with nothing more than an occasional grunt from her in response. Candle making must be exhausting.

"Good night, Gracie," I whispered in her ear. Then I snapped off the bedside light.

The Fort Kent Block House

EIGHT

Out, out brief candle!
Life's but a walking shadow, a poor player
That struts and frets his hour upon the stage . . .
—WILLIAM SHAKESPEARE, *MACBETH*

The summer wore away in inches, a gloriously long season, the way the summers of childhood used to be, with days so long and light-filled they seemed to have no end. Lydia finished her candle-making class, and so we didn't see much of Dee Dee for a couple of months. Candlemania, however, was loose in Fort Kent. The class had grown so large that it had to be held on two separate nights. *The St. John Valley Times,* our local paper, ran a story on the class, and Dee Dee's return to her roots. "Every woman in Fort Kent will have a house full of candles," the editor, Julia Bayly, predicted. This didn't surprise me. Our own house was filled with candles: floating candles, star-shaped candles, rose-shaped candles, twisted candles, candles that smelled of vanilla, candles that smelled of strawberry, candles that didn't smell at all, candles hanging to dry, candles already dried. As I predicted, Lydia and Dee Dee became fast friends—soul sisters, as Lydia described it.

Three days a week Trooper came to the clinic, still keeping up with his regular chores. As steady as a Swiss clock, he always turned up on Sunday afternoons, knowing that I would pay a visit to the Freebaker farm. The new colt was as fit and fine as a young horse could be. And while Clarence also had a herd of cows and other animals that I kept a close eye on, there really wasn't a need for me to stop by weekly. I did it mostly to enable Trooper to visit the colt. I knew the experience of seeing the animal born had cemented itself in his psyche and I wanted him to have the opportunity to see the little horse growing bigger, stronger. So each Sunday we stopped by the Freebaker farm and drank a lemonade as we watched the colt prance about the pasture. It was still sticking close to its mother, and yet fighting for its independence by playfully bolting a few feet away when the urge came upon it. I could tell that Clarence knew the regular visits were to appease the boy. And appease they did, for Trooper hung over the fence, transfixed at the sight of such grace atop four slender legs.

Trooper was also getting bold enough to watch me do neuters. And he had plenty of opportunity for it: More animals than ever were filing through the clinic. Even with Lyddie and me both hard at work, it seemed there was never a free moment. My evenings and Sundays were spent driving to neighboring farms, seeing that the farm animals were inoculated for the upcoming winter. Any spare minutes that happened to pop up were put toward overseeing the building of the new house, out on those fifty acres of good northern Maine soil.

Tourists paraded through town, stopping to click photos at the Fort Kent Block House, which had been built during the Aroostook War over the boundary dispute between the United States and Canada. Or they came to see the sign near the mouth of the international bridge, a sign that had been around for as long as I could remember: *Here begins Route One, which runs for 2,109 miles, ending in Key West, Florida.* July turned into August, and August into September. Before we knew it, autumn was pressing down on us with a fierce urgency. On my drives out to the local farms I noticed daily how the tamaracks were changing, their needles turning yellow as hay. And beneath leaves that were slowly evolving into reds and yellows, the trunks of the birches shone whiter than ever. The oaks and aspen followed suit as the days wore on. Squirrels scurried to and fro across front lawns, storing acorns and seeds with an eagerness that spoke of the long snowy months which lay just ahead. In the fields goldenrods stood dying on their stalks, and migrant birds blackened the sky overhead, flocks headed south for the winter.

And then, as if feeling the icy grip of that cold blanket that was already forming beneath the surface of the soil, everything slowed down again. The building contractor packed up his equipment and left our dream home to settle down into its bones for the winter, out on Gagnon Road. When spring returned, he would be back with his crew to complete the inside. The local potato farmers had finished with their harvest, but there was still the odor of potatoes in the air, that sweet rich smell of upturned earth before the snows come.

Life at the clinic returned to normal. We were well past those litter-bearing months and thus the flow of stray and unwanted animals had dwindled down to a trickle. Nature was telling us to stop and assess, to slow our own lives down a bit. That's when I realized just how long it had been since we had seen Dee Dee. I scolded myself for letting time get away, but I reasoned that Dee Dee was also busy, what with her little shop, a small son to raise, and then those popular candle-making classes. And Trooper, when asked, always said that his mother was fine.

It was early October and the maple in Dee Dee's front yard was running to pure scarlet by the time I drove up to 204 Bay Street again. I wish I could say I'd stopped by to check on her, but I hadn't. It took an emergency of sorts to jolt me out of the complacency that can descend on you when you live a busy life in the heart of a small, safe town. It began when Lydia came back from Paradis Shop & Save one evening, greatly distressed. She'd just run into Dee Dee. I was at my desk in the clinic, trying to catch up on the accounting that I'd let ride over the busy summer.

"Sam," Lydia said. "Now I'm *really* worried about Dee Dee. She doesn't look well at all. Oh, Sammy, I know something is terribly wrong." I was about to promise Lydia that I'd stop by 204 Bay Street first thing in the morning, on my way out to give Leroy Martin's mare a tetanus shot, when the phone rang at the clinic. It was Dee Dee. Had I seen Trooper anywhere? They'd had a fight, and she'd sent him up to his room. But now he was gone. She'd called all his friends. She'd driven up and down the streets of town several times. He was nowhere to be found, it was almost nine o'clock, and she was frantic.

"Don't worry," I told her. "I think I know where he might be."

An early autumn moon, three-fourths full and yellow as summer squash, was pulling itself up over the line of trees that edged the road out to Clarence Freebaker's farm. As I drove, two white-tailed deer shot out of the trees and flew across the path of my car, like ballet dancers leaping about the stage. But this is northern Maine, a place teeming with wildlife, and the best plan is to drive with caution. "We share this planet," I told Trooper many times during the course of our rides together. "It belongs to all living things, Troop. We need to respect them, too." I could only hope it would be the one notion I could safely instill in his young mind. And northern Maine is the best classroom for proof of how we need to share this little mound of rock, third in line from our own bright star. Before my headlights would pick up rough-board fence surrounding Clarence's lower pasture, I would also encounter a red fox, its two narrow eyes igniting like fire in my headlights as it slipped into a stand of tall hay for protection. The fox's appearance was later followed by a swift motion of owl wings, so fast and illusive that I could only surmise that it was a barred owl, out on its nightly hunt. And then my truck pulled out of the heavy conifers and into the flat pastureland of Clarence Freebaker's farm.

I went up to the front door before I went out to the barn. Clarence's wife answered my knock and I explained to her why I was suddenly on the premises on such a velvety October night.

"I've got a feeling he's with the colt," I told her. She nodded and smiled, just as Clarence appeared behind her shoulder.

"We'll just stay back here, out of the way," Ellen Freebaker told me. "You go on out to the barn." Clarence nodded agreement.

"The light switch is just inside the front door," he said, "on the right."

I would have used the light switch except that the moon had spilled in through the barn window, all over the hay, as though it were a silver milk from some magical cows owned by the Freebakers. It also lit up the horse stalls with a nice splash of light almost as powerful as the light from those candles so beloved by Dee Dee and her students. The smell of fresh hay, newly cut from that summer, hung in the air like a natural perfume. I stood for a minute, letting my eyes adjust further to the shapes and shadows before me, and that's when I saw him. Trooper Langford. Aged nine. He was lying on his side, one hand reaching out to touch the little colt that lay beside him, its head up, its legs curled beneath it. Trooper was sound asleep. I shook him gently, urging him awake. He sat up and rubbed his eyes, surprised to find me there peering down at him.

"Sam," he said, not a question, but a statement.

"You scared your mother to death," I told him, an edge of disappointment to my voice. I was pleased as hell to find him, but I didn't want him to think that I would condone such a trick as he'd just pulled on Dee Dee. "You can't run away each time you have a fight with your mom, Troop," I continued. "Or with anybody, for that matter. Now, come on,

125

I'll take you home. But you need to tell your mom that this won't happen again." He struggled to his feet, and so did the colt, still nervous at my sudden appearance, a disruption to the moonlighty stillness in the barn.

While Trooper situated himself in the truck, I went in to say good night to the Freebakers. Then Troop and I flew for home, his eyes tracing the dark outlines of trees that swept by his window, mine on the lookout for more deer and fox and whatever else nature might throw at me on this nightly drive through the country. After a mile or two, Trooper turned away from his window.

"Sam," he asked, "what happens to the dogs and cats at the clinic when, you know, when you give them that stuff that puts them to sleep? Do they ever wake up?" I was surprised, to say the least, but Lydia and I had anticipated that he would one day ask such questions. After all, the clinic was becoming part of his life and it was impossible to hide things from him. Impossible, and maybe even *wrong*.

"No, Troop," I finally answered. "Those animals don't wake up. We put them to sleep because they were very, very sick. Too sick to ever get well. And because the owners loved them so much, they were willing to spare them any more sickness." I took a deep breath. I could feel my heart doing a pitty-pat in my chest. Funny how kids can unnerve adults faster than anyone. Trooper thought long and hard about my statements.

"Where do those animals go when they die, Sam?" he asked now. "Do they go to the same place as people?" This one was tougher, and so I shrugged. I didn't want to present my beliefs to him as if they were the *only* beliefs to have. I had answers for *me,* but that didn't mean they were the right answers for Trooper.

"I don't know, Troop," I said with a sigh, hoping the sigh would quell his curiosity. This was Dee Dee's job, after all. Another minute passed, and I thought I was through with the inquisition. But I was wrong.

"Do you believe what Mom says?" Trooper was now asking. "Do you believe that every time we light a candle an angel is born?"

I shook my head. "I think your mother means it as nice poetry," I said. "But who's to say?"

"Sam?" The boy was relentless. What kind of a fight had he and Dee Dee had, anyway? "What happens when we die?" I felt my reserve slipping further and further away, for now he had hit the nail right on the head. He had gone for the Big Question. What to tell him? I had never considered myself a religious man, had always leaned more to the scientific. But this was a nine-year-old boy questioning me about life's greatest mystery. I knew I'd have to answer carefully. I took a deep breath as I planned my words. Ahead of me the bare potato fields turned yellow in my headlights, then rolled behind the truck into blackness.

"I don't know, Trooper," I told him. "I wish I did, but I just don't. There are people who believe that when we die we go to heaven to be with God. And when we do, we'll see everyone we ever loved up there, alive and well. And then there are some folks who believe that when we die, we just cease to be." Trooper thought about this, staring out his window at stars that had just broken through the clouds over the eastern sky. I had already turned off the Back Settlement road and onto Route 1 when he spoke again.

"I think Mom will go to heaven when she dies," he said at last. I looked over at him, his small body leaning against the door, his face pressed against the window. He was worried about his mom. He was a kid with only one parent. It made sense. I reached over and patted his leg, reassuring him as best I could.

"Lucky heaven," I said. "Before your mom is there an hour, she'll have all the angels making candles." He smiled at this, a sad smile. "But she's not going anywhere for a long, long time," I added.

Dee Dee's sign, *Bay Street Candles,* was still proudly displayed on the lawn when I pulled up. While I waited for Trooper to find his gloves on the floor of the truck, I stood for a moment and breathed

128

in the cold autumn air, trying to envision the storms in December and January that would sweep in from the Canadian plains to bury us alive. Then, I went up the steps, Trooper at my heels, and knocked on Dee Dee's door.

Her appearance stunned me. Those high and beautiful cheekbones, once her finest feature, were now too prominent because her face had grown so thin. Even her arms seemed frail as matchsticks. Catching my stare, she quickly grabbed a sweater and pulled it on.

"It's getting cold," she said, as if in explanation. "Winter will soon be upon us." I was willing to bet that Dee Dee was buried in some heavy winter coat when Lydia ran into her earlier that evening. Her whole demeanor suggested that she was hiding something from us, from the whole world. I waited as she sent Trooper on up the stairs to bed.

"What the hell is going on?" I asked her, in my *matter-of-fact-don't-give-me-any-bull* voice, a voice Dee Dee knew well. I meant business. Enough was enough. She nodded, as if conceding that she'd been caught at some secretive game.

"I'll go tuck the little nomad into bed," she said. "There's a bottle of wine in the kitchen. Get two glasses. The time has come for us to have an honest talk, Sammy. I've just been putting it off. That's all." Taking each step with careful deliberation, she disappeared up the stairs.

It seemed like hours before Dee Dee came back down from Trooper's bedroom. I sat in the parlor, waiting, sipping wine, staring at the flickering candles that filled the big bay window. When the tension seemed too tightly knotted in my stomach, I paced the floor, counting each step, back and forth, back and forth. Finally, when I heard her slow footfalls on the stairs, I poured a bit of wine into her glass and waited for her. She appeared in the door of the parlor, looking like a ghostly mirror image of the old Dee Dee. Where had she gone to so quickly? And how could I have become so busy with the trivia of life that I hadn't taken the time to notice? Where was Lydia? Ross? Some friends *we* are, I thought. I handed her a glass of wine.

"You know," said Dee Dee, "I've thought about this moment a million times, Sammy, especially at night when I'm lying in bed. I even wrote a little speech in my head, what to say to you. How to tell you. And yet, right now, I don't remember one word of what I planned to say." She slumped down on the sofa. Time passed between us, a short time, really, maybe only a minute, two minutes. But in some ways, our lives unreeled themselves like an old film: Dee Dee and I splashing in the galvanized tub; Dee Dee and I making valentine cookies, the kitchen splattered with flour; Dee Dee and I smoking our first cigarette, then coughing for an hour; Dee Dee and I graduating from the eighth grade; Dee Dee and

I practicing a song for our little band: the milestones of our lives, as elusive as raindrops. And I knew then, as I sat there and watched the candles twinkling like stars—flickering as if a strong, cold wind were passing through the parlor—that this was no surprise. Not really. It was at that moment that I admitted the truth to myself: *I'd always known that I'd lose her.* At first, I'd thought that Bobby's taking her away, stealing her from her family and friends and hometown, was the greatest loss. But I'd only been deluding myself. There had always been something floating between us, between Dee Dee and me, some cloudlike sixth sense that I could never put my finger on. It had always caught me unawares, over the course of our lives, of our growing-up years. We could be in the midst of the greatest joy, in the heart of one of life's biggest moments, and the truth would grip me. *Pay attention here,* the truth would whisper. *Pay attention to this life that has collided with yours.* Only with Dee Dee did I feel this. Never with Ross. Never with any other friend. Not even with Lydia. *Dee Dee Michaud.*

"It's serious, isn't it?" I heard myself say, and I was surprised at the sudden strength there in my voice. Where was it coming from? Dee Dee sighed, as if relieved that I was being strong, as if suddenly knowing that the time had come to lean on someone, someone she trusted. She nodded slowly.

"I'm dying, Sammy," she said. "Cancer." As quickly as that, with just a handful of words, Dee

131

Dee had put all her cards on the table for me to see. I don't know what I thought might happen at a moment like that. Would the room spin dramatically around and around? Would a montage of past experiences twirl before my eyes? For the first time in my life, words completely failed me. I could only stare, stare and remember, for behind Dee Dee's thin and shallow face I could still see the face of a twelve-year-old. *I want to be a revolutionary, Sammy. I want to be like those people in the song, fighting for liberty under the stars.* I felt my lips growing numb and tried to swallow, but I couldn't. It seemed as if my system was shutting down, too traumatized by this news. There had to be some answer, some specialist somewhere, some new treatment hovering on the horizon. I felt warm tears forming in my eyes. The curtains moved in the early autumn breeze that was wafting up from the river. The candles caught that breeze and reacted with a flickering dance. Dee Dee moved close to me, put her arms around my shoulders to comfort me. *She* was comforting *me!*

"It's okay, Sammy," she whispered. "I've already been down this road. I know what it's like. It's denial."

"It's not fair," I finally managed to say, but my throat felt as if it were wrapping itself around each word, clutching at them. I tried to breathe deeply as Dee Dee patted my back. I felt foolishly like a child being comforted by its mother. This should be the other way around, I thought. *I should be holding her.* What had happened to all that strength of a minute ago?

"It's just not *fair,*" I whispered again. Dee Dee actually smiled at this.

"Since when has the scientific-minded Sammy Thibodeau expected life to be fair?" she asked. She was right. I'd always said it was a shuffle of the cards. Some folks draw a bad hand. Some folks draw a few aces. "At least I was given time to take care of Trooper," Dee Dee continued. "To get him ready, to get him as safe as I can. Not every parent is given that chance, Sammy. Some are taken instantly. I asked God to give me time to see that Trooper is okay. And in return for that, I promised Him that I wouldn't leave this world in anger. In sadness, maybe, but not anger. And that's what God did, Sammy. He gave me *time,* which is a great gift." I wiped my eyes and looked over at her. I wanted to ask her what kind of God would do this to a *stranger,* much less one of His children. I wanted to ask her why God was the dealer of the cards in the first place. But I couldn't, for I saw in her face such concern, such love, that I realized all that mattered to Dee Dee now was her son. Dee Dee knew that the cards had already been shuffled out and the game was in full swing. It didn't matter anymore *who* was dealing.

"You told Trooper?" I asked, and Dee Dee nodded.

133

"He's very upset," she said. "I told him earlier this evening. I had to. It was time. That's why he's mad at me. That's why he ran away." I nodded. It all made sense to me now, Trooper's relentless questions about life and death, his dark, melancholy mood.

"He's got a lot of questions," I said. "And so do I." Dee Dee nodded. She swirled her red wine about, watching the colors explode on the inside of the glass. I filled my own glass again and waited.

"You were right about Bobby, of course," Dee Dee said. "He went from selling pot to harder drugs, getting worse as the years went by. Then, just after Trooper was born, Bobby went to jail for six months. When he got out he headed for Alaska, to work on the pipeline, or so he said. He promised to send us money, but we never got any. About two years after Bobby left, a policeman came to my door. He said Bobby had been killed in a drug deal gone bad. So you see, Sammy, it's always been just Trooper and me."

What had I been doing, in my own safe and stable life, while Dee Dee was trying to raise a young son alone? Studying for exams, most likely. Thinking that getting an A rather than a B was the most important issue on the planet. Dee Dee had never called anyone for help, no one that I knew of.

"Why didn't you tell me?" I asked. "Why did you just disappear like that?"

"It's hard to be so *wrong* in front of so many people," Dee Dee answered. "That's one of the bad things about little towns, Sam. You fail so openly. I was young and headstrong and wanted to prove to everyone that I was right in eloping with Bobby." I nodded. I knew about little towns. They're really just big families.

"I'm glad you came back," I said, and I discovered in that instant that I was able to smile. Dee Dee nodded, but she knew I was still waiting for the answer to the biggest question of all.

"I started getting tired," she said, "about a year ago. I put it off, the way many of us do. Then I finally went to a doctor. It's non-Hodgkin's lymphoma. Sort of like a cousin to Hodgkin's disease. Listen to this, Sammy. They call it NHL for short. When the doctor told me that, the first thing I said was, 'I'm dying from the *National Hockey League?*'" I tried to smile at her joke—knowing it might help her at this moment, knowing the humor was for my benefit—but I couldn't. I could only stare at her thin face as more questions raced through my mind.

"Can't you do something?" I asked. "We put men on the moon, for Chrissakes. Are you telling me there's nothing you can take?"

"It's rare, Sammy," she said. "Less than five percent of newly diagnosed cancer cases are NHL. It can be inherited, but I got mine *de novo*. In other words, I came down with it all on my own. It was just bad luck. But it's a cancer that hits only *young* men and women, so I try to look at the positive side. Hey, I guess I'm still young at thirty-three."

"Please don't," I said. I couldn't endure it. She reached over then and took my hand up in hers. She began counting off my fingers, one at a time, the counting game we did as kids, when we first learned our numbers. Now, it seemed as if we'd been counting off the years of her life, all those long summers ago, not knowing.

"It's widespread," Dee Dee said. "Lymph nodes, bone marrow, my liver." I closed my eyes. I couldn't be hearing this. She had come back to Fort Kent to finally live her life, the life she should have been living all along. Why was this happening?

"What about chemotherapy?" I heard myself finally ask, although I dreaded what the answer might be. Dee Dee shrugged.

"I've already had combination chemo, or more than one drug," she said, "which is what my doctors in Wyoming recommended. My NHL isn't low-grade, Sammy. It's intermediate, which means I had one shot at a cure. But I didn't go into complete remission, as the doctors hoped. Instead, I'm just getting sicker."

"There must be something else you could try," I insisted. After all, this was America, land of the cellular phone and cyberspace. Why wasn't there a technological answer floating around out there somewhere? Dee Dee nodded.

"I could try more chemo," she said. "I could even have a bone marrow transplant, among other things. But the cards are stacked against me, Sammy. At least this time. We're talking baldness, vomiting, possible transfusions, bleeding. And it would all be for nothing in the end. I'm dying, kiddo. End of story."

"But you have to *fight*," I insisted. "You have to have *courage*." Dee Dee smiled, forgiving me, I suppose, my inexperience. My ignorance. My pure love for her. Because those were the days before I knew what courage really was. Those were the days of my innocence.

"Sometimes, Sammy," she said, "the most courageous thing is not in fighting, but in knowing that the battle is over. But I gave it a hell of a shot. I want you to know that."

"How long?" I asked. My heart was stopping, I was certain of it, for I could feel it thumping, as if desperate to get out of my chest. I would die first, before Dee Dee Michaud. I would die from the shock of losing her.

"I was hoping to make it until March, for Trooper's tenth birthday," Dee Dee said. "But it's happening fast now, Sammy. I don't think I can hold on that long. Now there's night sweats. Stomach pain. I throw up more than I keep down. These days, I'm saying a prayer that I'll make it until Christmas." Dee Dee and her prayers! I wanted to tell her to wake up, that prayers weren't going to save her now. Where had her prayers gotten her in the first place? I wanted to hit someone, *something,* I wanted to strike out at the unfairness of it all because, yes, damnit, it was *unfair.* It was heartless and cruel and inhuman. That's exactly what it was: *inhuman.* So maybe Dee Dee's God had caused it after all.

I watched the whimpering candles, for that's what they seemed to be doing, *whimpering,* their fingers of light washing up and down the walls of the parlor. The world was growing ugly, suddenly. The world was growing mean. But hadn't I always suspected that of the world? I'd just been living in a safe little cocoon, is all.

"I came back to Fort Kent hoping to get Trooper settled into a new life," Dee Dee continued. "I came back hoping to find the right couple to raise him. You were always my first choice, Sammy, always so logical and grounded. And I knew whoever you married would be the same. You and Lydia would be the best of parents." It took a few seconds for her words to register. Lydia and me. Me and Lydia. She was asking us to take her son. She was asking us to be Trooper's new mom and dad!

"Parents?" I repeated. Dee Dee nodded.

"You're the closest that boy has ever come to

having a father, Sam," she said. "And Lydia would make a perfect mom." I thought about her words, about that little boy growing up without her, without Dee Dee there to guide him. The book of their lives together shouldn't have been written this way. Dee Dee should have been in the bleachers for all those basketball games that were sure to come. She should have been there for baseball, and that first prom, and then college graduation, and then for the grandbabies, blood of her blood. She should have been given a spot in the background of Trooper's life, like some silent oak, well rooted and watching the progress of her only son.

"I'd be honored," I said. Then I looked at Dee Dee, my childhood comrade, my first love. "I'll talk to Lydia, tonight, when I get home."

With that assurance in hand, Dee Dee stood. I could see that she was very tired, for this had been an emotional time between us, a draining time. "But you have to promise me something, too," I said. She listened intently. "No more secrets," I added, "at least no secrets between you and us."

"It's a promise," Dee Dee said, and with that I hugged her good night, hugged her frail little body as tightly to me as I dared. Then I went outside, into the chilly October night, and jumped into my truck. I tried not to think as I started the engine and backed out of Dee Dee Michaud's drive, the one next to my old childhood home, a place so rife with memories that they grew thick from every tree, every shrub. A place where memories dripped like rain from the downspouts, flew like birds out of the chimney. A house full of remembrance.

I had to get away as fast as I could. But before I turned the corner at the end of the street, I took one last look in my rearview mirror. There was the big front window at 204 Bay, still afire with candles, candles that were glimmering with life. But it was a *backward* picture, a picture seen through my mirror, as if it were Alice's crazy looking glass, a place where now nothing was real. At least, I hoped it wasn't real. I hoped that in the morning, when the ragged October sun rose over the mountain behind the river, turning Fort Kent and Clair, New Brunswick, as yellow as old wheat, it would have been just a long and painful dream, this talk of Dee Dee's dying. I pushed the accelerator pedal down and sped away, as fast as I could, as if maybe sheer speed could lift me away from the truth and shuttle me forward, ahead of the flood. Now it all made sense: Dee Dee's frailty; her talk to Trooper about lighting candles for those times when she wouldn't be there; her eagerness that Trooper and I spend time together. As in a crazy soap opera with a million plots, all the threads to the story were suddenly weaving themselves together. Dee Dee had had a plan all along.

I turned into my own driveway at the clinic and sat there in the truck. I could see Lydia through the yellow window of the office as she worked on papers at the desk, her head tilted forward and resting on one hand as she read. I was overcome with love for her, but at the same time I knew that I could never keep her safe. Just as I could never keep Dee Dee safe, or Trooper safe, because we are all mortals caught up in the wash of fate, or the wash of just plain *bad luck*. What was the Latin Dee Dee had used? *De novo*. Some of us get hit first. Nothing personal. I was suddenly overcome with the knowledge of my own helplessness, and with it came a wave of such great remorse that I could no longer hold back the tears. So I sat there in my truck, my head on the steering wheel, and I wept. I knew that I would have to be strong for Trooper, for Dee Dee, for Lydia. And I was willing to do that, willing to do my duty. But just then, for just that moment in time as I sat in the dark outside my clinic, I would mourn my own great loss. Losing Dee Dee to Bobby Langford was one thing. I could still take comfort in the thought that she was somewhere on the earth, still being Dee Dee Michaud, still sounding as if she had just stepped out of the carefree sixties. But losing her to eternity was another matter. *De novo*. In my scientific mind that meant losing her forever, because I didn't see the world through Dee Dee's eyes. I didn't look at a candle—which was a lump of beeswax or paraffin—and see a goddamned guardian angel looking back at me. And then I thought of Bobby Langford, Trooper's good-looking, sweet-talking father, who would never know the great kid he and Dee Dee had created one innocent night, a life they had shaped, like one of Dee Dee's candles.

I cried for us all. Then I wiped my eyes and went inside to congratulate Lydia. After all, she and I were about to become parents for the first time.

Dee Dee's old bicycle

NINE

*I love thee to the level
of every day's most quiet need,
by sun and candle light*
—ELIZABETH BARRETT BROWNING,
FROM ONE OF DEE DEE'S CANDLE BOXES

*And so it came to be that the orbit of Dee Dee Michaud's
life had once again collided with mine. With Lydia's.
And, in doing so, it would cause our two lives to col-
lide with that of a frightened nine-year-old boy.
There is no reason to the universe. Just random acci-
dents. But you couldn't tell Dee Dee that. Not only
did she think some intelligent hand was guiding
everything, she saw no trouble in helping to steer that
intelligent hand. That was Dee Dee.*

As much as Lydia was devastated by the news of
Dee Dee's illness, she took strength from the knowledge that she and I could help the horrible situation
by raising Trooper as our own. Dee Dee could rest
easy on that issue. Lydia had come to love that boy
as much as I had. But it was hard to think of the joy

which lay ahead of us as Trooper's parents when we knew that we would lose Dee Dee in the process. Yet I was the one who had the harder time accepting the truth. In the days that followed I moved through my usual chores like an unfeeling ghost, a mere presence that offered its medical expertise to the pets of Fort Kent, Maine. I kept thinking that, surely, at some turn in the road, at some juncture in the day's events, acceptance would descend upon me. Maybe I would be suturing a cut paw, or extracting a piece of broken glass, or operating to remove a tumor, only to look up and say, "Hey, it's no big deal. We all gotta go someday. *Que sera, sera.*" But that never happened.

Along with the ghost I'd become, other ghosts paraded the streets of Fort Kent, Maine, when Halloween finally arrived at the end of the month. Large orange pumpkins sat on all the porches, some smiling out at the street as snaggle-toothed jack-o'-lanterns, others with glaring faces drawn by colored markers. For the occasion, Trooper dressed as a one-eyed, peg-legged sailor, having just read *Treasure Island* at school. We were rather proud of his choice of costume, considering that many of the older boys had chosen to dress as Arnold Schwarzeneggers and tote machine guns at their sides. At least, we were proud until we learned that Joan St. Amant, Trooper's fourth-grade teacher, had suggested that it might be a grand idea if the class chose their costumes from the subjects they were currently studying. So a steady stream of trick-or-treaters filtered in and out of the clinic all afternoon, Madonna and Bruce Willis might be immediately followed by Ben Hur and Betsy Ross, depending upon whether or not the student had taken Mrs. St. Amant's advice. Lydia and I were kept busy filling the huge glass candy bowl on the clinic's front counter.

"Don't eat too much candy," Lydia told Trooper, when he made his second visit to the candy bowl, Randy Cloutier looming at his side as Abraham Lincoln. "Remember that we've got the party later at your house, with lots of cake and ice cream."

"I wish we had a sick parrot at the clinic," I heard Trooper tell Randy as they went out the door. "I bet Sam would let me carry it around on my shoulder." I had to smile at this, imagining what the owner of a sick parrot might think if he looked out his window to see it traipsing down the street on Long John Silver's shoulder.

"What time is the party?" I asked Lydia. We were to go to Dee Dee's house that evening for more than just a Halloween party. Dee Dee had gotten it into her head that legal papers weren't enough to confirm that Lydia and I would adopt Trooper. She wanted a *candle ceremony,* as she called it, with candles and balloons and cake, and God only knew what else. "We live with rituals," Dee Dee told Lydia and me when

147

she first concocted the idea. "Rituals help us pass from one stage of our lives to another. I want Trooper to feel that he's totally involved in this important decision." Lydia loved the idea, but, truthfully, it scared the daylights out of me. A *candle ceremony?* Just what the hell might *that* be? I had complained vociferously to Lydia, beginning on the very day that the two women began laying plans for a Halloween party that would also double as an adoption ritual. (Tell *that one* to Miss Manners.) But I had complained to deaf ears. To Lydia, everything Dee Dee spoke was akin to gospel. Yet, now that Halloween had finally arrived, I tried again.

"You don't know Dee Dee like I do," I said to Lydia, still hoping to wring some common sense out of the issue. "Before we know it, she'll have us sitting inside miniature pyramids and listening to Yanni." But Lydia was not to be deterred.

"That sounds like fun," she said. I sighed as I stood in the window of the clinic and watched Long John Silver walking down a street in northern Maine, with Abraham Lincoln gamboling along at his side, a sight you might think you'd live your whole life without ever seeing. I felt Lydia next to me just then, felt her hand slide around my waist.

"It's important to *her,* Sam," Lydia said softly. "And right now, that's what really counts." I nodded, then leaned over to kiss my wife's forehead.

"I suppose," I said.

148

"Besides, what harm can a candle do?" Lydia asked as she gathered up her purse and keys. She had promised to stop by Dee Dee's early, to help with the preparations. I had to scoff at this. *What harm can a candle do?*

"Ha!" I said. "Just ask Mrs. O'Leary's cow that question." I waited, certain I had her on this one.

"I believe it was a *lantern* the cow kicked over," Lydia replied, and smiled facetiously. "Not a candle."

"Whatever," I said as she closed the door behind her.

I had some errands to run before the party. And since Lydia had promised to go early, I would have time to pull off what I hoped would be two great surprises: one for Trooper and one for Dee Dee. And Lydia would be surprised in the cross fire, for she never thought I could effectively keep a secret from her. But I had. As a matter of fact, over the past week, I'd done a lot of clandestine work. And it had paid off. Despite my reservations about a candle ceremony, I was looking forward to seeing Dee Dee's and Trooper's faces when they realized that I had tricks *and* treats up my sleeve.

As had come to be expected of anyone who visited Dee Dee Michaud, the whole front window at 204 Bay was breathing with candles, an undulating sea of firelight. Dee Dee answered the door, gleeful and happy, considering the circumstances. She looked almost radiant, but I knew that she had tricks of her own up the sleeves of that flowing blue gown she was wearing. I suspected it was makeup and not just radiance that was suddenly hiding her pale skin. But she was unflappable, as usual. And atop her hair sat a small rhinestone tiara.

"I'm a princess, Sammy," she said happily, as she twirled slowly, showing off the billowy gown. I gave her my best and bravest smile.

"Tell me something I don't know," I replied.

"Ross and Vickie are already here," Dee Dee said. "In the kitchen." I glanced one last time out at my truck, to the black tarp in the back that covered my surprise. Then I went in to the kitchen, where Ross was already popping the top off a cold beer for my benefit.

Dee Dee had invited a dozen or so other guests, old acquaintances and new, mostly all students from her candle-making class. These were people who had been told about her illness. But I knew that Dee Dee couldn't hide such a physical thing as cancer from the other residents of a small town. No doubt rumors were already circulating. And that's why Lydia and I had advised Dee Dee to just let people know the truth, especially now that it was really the only choice. Her privacy could be contained no longer.

By the time everyone finally arrived—including Long John and Honest Abe—Ross had already set up a couple of amps and microphones. There had been several pleas from friends earlier in the week for an encore of the Acute Angles, a command performance, if you will. And now Ross was playing a tune on his acoustic guitar, getting ready for our big moment. Every now and then, when Dee Dee and I passed by, we leaned down to the mike and sang a bit of harmony with him. It was like old times, all right. One could almost imagine we were all safe, there in the lilting house at 204 Bay Street, that we were suddenly wrapped in gauze, the kind I use at the clinic to bind cuts. But I knew the truth: All humans live and love and die without a safety net. Sometimes, you can't bind your wounds. And that fact somehow makes us *all* heroic.

"Okay, gang," Dee Dee said, clapping her hands for attention. "It's time to make the candles. That way, they'll be dry for the ceremony."

We gathered in the doorway of her small workroom, sipping wine and beer, and munching from plates of sandwiches and other goodies. I watched closely as Dee Dee turned on the burner beneath her big double boiler. I was surprised to find the process even mildly interesting, but it was. First, the wax in the boiler began to heat, and then melt, moving in little swirls. I stepped aside to make room for Vickie and Lydia and Diane Morneault, who were crowding in next to me. I wondered what might happen next, for, in truth, I'd never seen a candle made before. For all I knew, candles were grown on *candlenut* trees in Kentucky. I looked around the room and saw shelf after shelf of candles, all wrapped in soft tissue, and I assumed that these were the ones Dee Dee sold to the public. I could also see nails driven into the walls of the room and wondered what tortures lay ahead for the paraffin.

"This looks like a scene from *House of Wax*," I heard Ross whisper in my ear, his breath smoky. "Is Vincent Price here?"

When the wax was finally heated, Dee Dee motioned for Trooper and me to step forward. As we did, she took a long white wick from a drawer.

"Now, each of you take hold of the wick's middle," she instructed us. "That way, you'll each have an end to dip. Dipped candles are made a pair at a time," she explained, when she saw my questioning look. As Trooper and I both held our wick at its middle, Dee Dee helped guide our hands and we carefully dipped the ends into the heated wax.

"Now," she said happily. "Pull the ends out and wait for three minutes. See? That's your first layer." And so it was. Then, she instructed us to repeat the process. We kept adding layers in this fashion until the candles were as thick as Dee Dee wanted them.

"What now?" I asked, wondering if Troop and I would be compelled to hold the things while they dried. I didn't see any fun in *that*.

"We need to keep the pair apart," Dee Dee

152

answered. "Like this." And she hung the two candles, still joined by the wick, over two nails. "That will keep them separate until they're dried," she added.

Then it was Lydia's and Trooper's turn. Lydia, of course, knew from all those classes exactly what to do. She looked like a pro. And while I never thought I'd feel proud that my wife was adept at making a candle, I *was* proud. She and Trooper applied layer after layer until they, too, had made a perfect pair of candles, still joined by the wick. They hung their candles next to the first pair to dry.

"Now, we need to wait an hour, until they're dried," Dee Dee said.

The small crowd moved back into the kitchen, and then on to the parlor. It was obvious by this time that the Acute Angles, bless our aging hearts, could no longer avoid the requests from our friends to sing a song. So Dee Dee and I positioned ourselves, one on each side of Ross, and, doing the best we could after years of not rehearsing together, we sang for our friends. Dee Dee had chosen the song earlier, one of her favorites that our band used to play.

"If I know Dee Dee," said Diane Morneault, herself a member of a local band called High Fidelity, "the song is by either ABBA or Van Morrison." She was right. It was the latter. The Acute Angles had pretty much been Van Morrison groupies back in the seventies. If I had a penny for every time I sang

"Brown Eyed Girl," or for every time I heard it on some oldies station on the radio and thought of Dee Dee, I'd be a rich man. I could close down my practice overnight. Before we actually did the song, however, I had a few words I wanted to say.

"This song is for Brian," I told our listeners, "wherever he may be right now." Dee Dee and Ross nodded their approval. Brian LeBlanc had been the fourth member of our group until he moved away from Fort Kent. Brian, with the perpetual smile, who died in his car at the age of twenty-seven when a drunk driver ran a red light.

The song, "Into the Mystic," with its talk of foghorns calling our gypsy souls home, was definitely for Brian. I wished he were still with us, beating away on his drums behind the three of us. But he wasn't. He would never be again.

When we sang, shaky as it was, it all came back. And Christ, it felt good! It felt like *immortality,* is what it felt like, the three of us singing again. I could almost feel Brian behind us, as if he were still right there, the steady beat of his drums guiding us along. I know Dee Dee felt it, too, and so did Ross. Once, I even turned and looked behind me. Ross winked when he saw this, and Dee Dee smiled. They knew; they felt him, too. Good old Brian, whose soul and spirit had already flown into the mystic. I wished the night could last forever. But I knew it wouldn't.

That's not the way the cards are dealt. Soon there would be just Ross and me left to sing the Oldies but Goodies.

We finished to a round of cheers and solid applause. Bless our friends. We could always count on a dozen CDs selling, if some executive ever got drunk enough to sign us up to a record label. Dee Dee was shining. I reached out and took her hand, squeezed it. Ever the romantic, Ross went out on the back porch for a cigarette.

"Don't be gone long," Dee Dee shouted after him. "The ceremony is about to begin." And so it was, for the newborn candles were dry. Dee Dee carried them in to the front parlor as Trooper and I exchanged one of our "guy" looks behind her back. After all, there seemed to be a lavish interest in candles, a bit too much for a couple of scientific souls like us. And Ross apparently agreed. He'd already flashed us a few *can you believe this?* looks of his own.

"Sam and Trooper will go first," Dee Dee announced. She took the pair of candles we had made—they were still joined by the wick—and gave one to each of us. I had to smile when I saw that my hand was shaking. I was never very good at public performances. At our eighth-grade graduation I had frozen in my chair from just hearing my name called out. To a great wave of laughter rolling in from the audience, Dee Dee had gone up and received my diploma for me. Then she had shoved it into my hand until my fingers could finally grasp it and hold on. I'd been teased about this for years.

Now Dee Dee took a pair of scissors out of a cabinet and positioned them at the center of the wick, ready to snip.

"It's just like an umbilical cord, isn't it?" she asked gleefully.

"I'm gonna barf," Trooper said, and rolled his eyes backward.

"Me too," I said, and rolled my own eyes for effect. At least until Lydia frowned at me. Then Dee Dee looked down at Trooper, up at me. As if everyone in the room sensed the change in mood, the atmosphere grew somber, respectful.

"Until we meet again," Dee Dee said softly, "I lend you my son." And then, with her friends watching closely, she cut the wick, separating the two candles. Now, I held my own, as did Trooper. Suddenly, I was overcome with emotion. It no longer seemed a funny joke between the guys. This was serious business, this act of delivering a child into the care of others. I swallowed hard, desperately trying to remain stoic as Lydia and Trooper took up their own pair of candles and held them while Dee Dee cut that wick, too. I could see that Lydia's eyes were brimming with moist tears.

"Until we meet again," Dee Dee said to Lydia, "I lend you my son." Dee Dee now took the extra candle from Trooper. "Now we each have one," she said. "It's time to light them." Ross came forward with his perpetual matches, and, as Dee Dee, Lydia, Trooper, and I held out our candles, he lit them for us. Under further instruction from Dee Dee, we left the four candles burning brightly on a table in the parlor. I leaned down and hugged Trooper to me, then Dee Dee. Lydia did the same. We would raise Trooper for Dee Dee Michaud, our friend, and he had been part of the decision, the transition. It was the best we could do. The candle ceremony was over.

Now it was time to change the somber and quiet atmosphere. Dee Dee had wanted this to be a night of celebration. She'd said so time and time again to Lydia and me. "I hope no one is sad," she had said, "at least not for long." So it was a perfect time for the two surprises I was still keeping in my pocket. The first would be for Trooper. He came forward when I called for him, his Long John Silver eye patch now missing.

"Yeah, Sam?" he asked.

"In honor of the occasion," I announced, "this is for you." Then I handed him an envelope, which he tore open. "It's your Christmas present, a little early," I added, as Trooper held up a Polaroid shot of the Freebaker foal. At the top of the picture I'd written the words: *Trooper's First Horse.* He was thrilled, his face smiling around the sad eyes that he'd been looking at the world with for the past few days.

"Ah, man! Look at this!" he shouted to Randy. "My own horse!"

"When the new house is finished out on Gagnon Road," I said, "we'll have a little barn for him." Lydia came over to give me a peck on the cheek. "And we'll fence that small pasture for him. He'll stay at Clarence's in the meantime." Trooper threw his arms around my waist and gave me a quick hug, just the right amount of affection in front of Randy. And then he started making the rounds of the guests, showing everyone the photo of his new horse. When the picture finally reached Dee Dee I saw first a sweet sadness on her face. *I won't see him ride his first horse.* And then a smile covered her sadness, placed there for Trooper. After all, Dee Dee herself had declared that this night would be a joyful one.

"It's beautiful, Troop," Dee Dee said. She looked over at me then, gave me one of those piercing looks that could run right down to the root of your soul. I knew what she was feeling, because I was feeling it, too. We were all good friends gathered for a special occasion, gathered to take care of a child as best we could. But one of us was going to die. The Yin and Yang of life.

Ross put a CD on the stereo, one that he had brought with him: *ABBA's Greatest Hits.*

"For you, my lady," he told Dee Dee.

"I knew it!" she exclaimed gleefully. "I asked God to make this an ABBA night, and He did!" She tousled Ross's hair, a thing he truly hated, and then disappeared into the parlor. Ross leaned toward me, his hand to his mouth in an effort to talk privately.

"When Dee Dee mentions God," he asked, "do you think of a cross between Casey Kasem and Dr. Ruth?" I nodded.

"New Age stuff," I answered. "You know. God as a caring next-door neighbor, God as your best friend. Only trouble is, you better cover your back and lock your door."

"Man, you are *so* cynical," Ross said, approvingly.

"I know," I answered. "Isn't it wonderful?"

Through the aura of sadness that had hung over the evening, there was so much *life* in the house—the kind of life that Dee Dee Michaud brought into rooms wherever she went—with candles lighting up the front parlor, with companionship, laughter, heritage. It would be easy to believe that Dee Dee would be safe after all, that she would always be in the house at 204 Bay Street, selling her lovely candles and listening to ABBA. But my scientific mind knew better. I whispered to Lydia that she was to get Dee Dee and meet me on the front porch.

"Another surprise?" Lydia asked. "*Et tu, Brute?* Where was I when this was all going down?" I shrugged.

"See how easy it would be for me to have an affair?" I asked, and then I slipped out the front door.

The autumn air smelled sharply of winter, the way it can in northern Maine. A sprinkling of stars erupted over the mountain on the Canadian side, free from even the tiny bit of light pollution that hovers over Fort Kent. I lowered the tailgate of the pickup and jumped up into the back of the truck. I took the tarp off the shiny blue bicycle that was lying flat on its side, and then carefully lifted the bike down. Taking it by the handlebars, I pushed it over to the front porch and stood there waiting for Dee Dee and Lydia to appear. When they did, Dee Dee's face registered first surprise, and then recognition: *her old bike, her last bike, the one she had forsaken for womanhood.*

"But I sold that to Jimmy Desjardins!" Dee Dee exclaimed. "Over twenty years ago!" With Lydia behind her, and still wearing the blue princess gown and tiara, Dee Dee came down the steps and took the handlebars from me.

"Jimmy sold it to Rick Levasseur," I said. "Rick painted it red, and when he was done using it, he gave it to Benny Pelletier." Dee Dee looked up at me in complete awe, as though it were a history of England I was unreeling there in the night. "Benny painted it black, and then tore the seat open in a rather nasty bike accident, when he collided with the Fish River Bridge. So it went into the Pelletier barn when it should have gone into a bike hospital."

"How did you finally find it?" Dee Dee asked, as

she slid a leg over the seat and sat down on her old bike, the very one she'd mentioned that spring, when she and Trooper first came to dinner to meet Lydia. *I'd give anything to have that bike back,* she'd said.

"I asked Vernon Pelletier if he'd look in his barn, and sure enough, there it was, covered with cobwebs and scratched to the high heavens. So I took it over to Louie's Auto Repair and asked Louie what he could do to fix it. We matched the original paint pretty well, I think. And Louie's sister Lana redid the leather on the seat."

"It's perfect," Dee Dee breathed. "It's just like new. It's my bike, all right. Oh, Sammy, you think of everything, don't you? This has been such a wonderful night." And then, to our own surprise, she tucked the gown in around her legs as best she could.

"You're not thinking what I think you are?" Lydia asked. "You're not seriously thinking of riding that thing, are you?" Dee Dee looked over at us, the same mischievous smile I'd seen a million times from childhood.

"Why the hell not?" she asked, and then she was gone, down Bay Street, her gown flapping from the sides of the bike, and the streetlights lighting up all the rhinestones in her tiara.

"Sam," Lydia protested. "She shouldn't be riding a bike, sick as she is. I don't think this is good for her."

I just smiled, shrugged. Dee Dee shouldn't be *dying,* that's what she shouldn't be doing. So how was a little biking going to hurt?

"She's still alive, Lyddie," I said. "Let's just let her live the way she wants to." From the end of Bay Street we heard a loud whoop of joy as Dee Dee turned the corner and disappeared.

"Where does she find the strength?" Lydia wondered, as she reached over and tugged at my earlobe, her own little way of saying she loved me, even if I sometimes drove her crazy.

"I think there's strength in numbers," I answered. "At least for tonight, there's strength in having us all here."

"The bike was a great idea," Lydia added. "Did you see her face?" I nodded. Then I looked up again at the dark sky that seemed to be painted above the Canadian side of the river.

"The weathermen say there's snow heading our way," I said, hoping to change the subject. The truth was that the bicycle would eventually go to Trooper, and then, well, maybe it would go into the barn we would build for the foal, and it would wait there, covered in cobwebs, until Trooper's son needed a bike. But kids wanted updated models of things these days. Kids weren't into antiques. Maybe the bike would be something like a centerpiece, a reminder of a sweet, soft life that had flown through ours like a migrating bird.

"Let's go back inside before Ross eats all the food," Lydia whispered, sensing my sadness, no doubt. So I put my arm around her waist, and we went back inside the house at 204 Bay Street, in search of another piece of cake.

Sliding above town

TEN

I shall light a candle of understanding in thine heart, which shall not be put out.
—APOCRYPHA (VULGATE)

Two days after the candle ceremony, Dee Dee came to our apartment above the clinic to help set up a room for Trooper. After a discussion of tactics with Lydia—I'd begun to call them the general and the sergeant at arms—Dee Dee felt that Trooper would have an easier time making the transition from his place to ours if she were there to help out. It made perfect sense, difficult as it was, but if I had had my way, I would have put Dee Dee's dying far into the back of my mind until the inevitable was rapping at my door. But I knew in my gut she was right. "I don't want to wait until I die," she told me, "and then have him taken out of his own house and into yours. I want him to feel like your house is already home." So, weak as she'd become, Dee Dee had begun helping

165

Trooper set up what would be his new room, in his new house, in his new life. They began by hanging posters on the wall, Troop's favorite movie stars and athletes, and arranging some of his clothes in the closet. They had started early in the morning, and when I came up from the clinic for lunch, I listened to their chatter as I ate.

"When you guys move out to Gagnon Road, to the new house," Dee Dee was asking, "what colors do you want for your room?"

"Purple," said Trooper. "I think purple is really cool."

"You know," I heard Dee Dee say, "I'm going to leave that one for Lydia to deal with, Troop." I had to smile. It was true that I'd disapproved of this latest tactic at first, but listening to the two of them now, I realized that this would be better for Trooper. This was probably the way nature intended it: We should prepare for death as though it's some important visitor. *The son of a bitch.*

When I'd finished my lunch and put the dishes in the sink, I went to Trooper's room—what we had been calling *the spare bedroom*—and leaned against the door to watch. Arnold Schwarzenegger was on one wall, Garth Brooks on another. I imagined that in a short time some sexy little Hollywood vixen and a hot country music songstress would replace these two masculine posters. Plastic model cars sat on the dresser, next to a football and a couple of books of baseball stats. The curtains and bedspread were now solid greens and browns, and not the light puffy things that Lydia had put there when we first moved in.

"Looks good," I said, nodding my approval at the changes before me. Trooper smiled.

"Thanks, Sam," said Dee Dee. "But be warned that Troop wants purple walls in the new house." I nodded, pretending to be nonchalant about it. And pretending not to notice how much more frail and thin Dee Dee seemed to be, in just the two days following her now famous candle ceremony.

"At least the walls will match Lydia's eggplant casserole," I said.

"There are worse things than purple things, anyway," said Trooper.

"Yeah?" said Dee Dee. "What?" Trooper thought a bit.

"Lime things?" he asked. Dee Dee shrugged.

"You may be right," she said.

"Sam?" Trooper asked, and I could tell by his voice that something out of the ordinary was on its way. "Mr. Finley asked our class how many angels can dance on the head of a pin. We're supposed to answer the question on Monday. So how many, Sam?" I smiled, catching Dee Dee's knowing eye.

"I think it's one of those questions, Troop, where

the answer really doesn't matter," I said, "because it's a question that can't be argued." Dee Dee didn't like my answer. She raised her hand.

"My turn," she said. "I know how many angels can dance on the head of a pin. As many as care to dance." Trooper smiled. My answer had obviously fallen short, so I tried again.

"Okay, how about this?" I offered. "The answer is one. Your mom." Dee Dee threw a pillow in my direction, and I ducked.

"Hey, look!" said Trooper, pointing at the window. I glanced in the direction of his finger and saw what those weathermen had been predicting: a million fat fresh snowflakes, swirling around and around in the cold air like small white feathers. It was snowing. Our first snowfall of the season. Dee Dee lifted herself carefully from the edge of the bed and went to the window.

"Look, Troop," she said as he joined her there. "Snowflakes. No two are alike. Just like candles. Just like angels."

"You mean there are no twin angels?" I asked. "No triplets? That could spoil a lot of fantasies for us guys."

"Bye, Sam," said Dee Dee. I could take a hint.

"You two have fun decorating," I said. "I got a clinic to run."

"What did Sam mean about the triplets, Mom?" I heard Trooper ask. I left them there at the window—

discussing snowflakes, and angels dancing on pins—
and I went back down to the clinic.

By midafternoon, four inches of snow had piled
up over Fort Kent, so intent was our first storm of
the season in making itself known. Cancellations
had poured in to the clinic from the folks who lived
on the outreaches of town, on the twisty back
roads. By early afternoon the snowplow had already
been out a couple of times. It had scraped and
banged its way past the clinic, its yellow lights flash-
ing as it went. I was just about to make a few orders
when I looked up and saw Dee Dee, her head stuck
around the door of my office. She pretended to
knock.

"You busy?" she asked. I shook my head.

"Come on in," I told her. She sat in a chair in front
of my desk and looked my little office over with a
great intensity. She was obviously still in a decorating frame of mind.

"You know," she said, after a time, "this clinic
might be the best place for my AƎBA poster." I
frowned.

"I'm hoping to bring clients *in*," I said. Dee Dee
nodded. She pointed at the wall behind the office
door.

"But if it hung right *there*," she said, "no one would
see it when your office door was open." She looked
at me and smiled.

"But I would see it when the door was closed," I protested.

"I know," Dee Dee said, that mischievous grin back on her face. "That's the whole point, Sammy. I like the idea of you seeing my poster when you're in here alone. It's a collector's item, you know." I shook my head, trying to envision a lifetime of staring at AƎBA each time I craved some peace and quiet.

"How'd it go with Trooper's room?" I asked.

"We stopped for today because I have a favor to ask," said Dee Dee. Then she gave me her famous *please, please, please* look, one that had always leveled me in a matter of seconds.

"What?" I asked, trepidation in my voice.

"I want to go sliding, Sammy," she pleaded. "Like we did when we were kids. I haven't been sliding since I was twelve years old. I want to go sliding with you, and Lydia, and Trooper."

"Dee Dee," I said, my voice the stern voice of a doctor who must suddenly play God and Dad all at the same time. "The bike incident was one thing, but there comes a time when we have to recognize our limitations." Dee Dee was affecting a serious listening look all this time, her chin in one hand as she stared at me, her eyebrows up in mock concern. "It's not funny," I continued. "You're too sick to go sliding."

"Okay, Doc," she said. She dropped her hand away from her chin and just sat there, saying nothing, defeated. I listened as the clock ticked away on the wall, then turned to look out the window. Snow was still falling, fat and sticky, the kind of snow that gives life to snowmen, and well-packed snowballs. I had a sled, one that Lydia and I bought during our first winter together in Fort Kent. Ross also had a sled, and an old-fashioned Flying Saucer. Did kids today even know what Flying Saucers are? Did they think they're ships that crashed in Roswell, New Mexico? Trooper would probably love the Flying Saucer.

"We should probably call Ross and Vickie," I said softly. Dee Dee sprang from the chair, full of sudden energy, and came around the desk to give me a big hug.

"Ross and Vickie are on their way over with a sled and a Flying Saucer," she announced. "And Lydia is getting your sled, and Troop is gathering up mittens and scarves. Can you be ready in five minutes?" And then she was gone.

I sat behind my desk, still unable to follow her, at least not yet. I looked at the blank wall behind my office door, tried to envision a six-foot-tall poster of ABBA hanging there, four faces looking at me every morning, faces that would never grow older, just as Dee Dee's face would never grow older, at least not in my memory of her. Not even after my own face began to look exactly like my father's, then my grandfather's, as I moved down the years of my life.

Dee Dee and AꓭBA would remain eternally young. *I must remember to get some of those hooks for hanging heavy posters,* I thought as I went out to lock the front door and get my coat and gloves.

Ross and Vickie were already waiting at the top of Daigle Hill by the time the four of us arrived. Randy had gone to Portland to visit his mother, so Lydia and Trooper doubled up and went first on our sled, followed by Vickie and Ross on theirs. Dee Dee and I stood, our breaths bursting out on the cold air in puffs of frozen vapor, and watched the two sleds disappear in streaks down the hillside, the wild cries of the sliders growing fainter and fainter. Then we heard excited whoops rise up from the bottom of the hill as the sleds arrived safely.

"I'm only going to go once," Dee Dee said. "I really just want to watch Trooper having fun like this." I nodded. I would wait, too, not wanting to leave her alone on the hilltop. So we sat on a fallen log and watched the others take a second and then a third turn down the hill. Looking out at the St. John Valley from our high perch, I was reminded of "The French Song," the one from our childhoods. While we waited for the others to climb the hill a fourth time, I began to sing, softly at first.

"Quand le soleil dit bonjour aux montagnes," I sang, my words solidified on the crisp air, *"et que la nuit rencontre le jour."* Dee Dee smiled, then joined in, singing

with me words written a couple hundred years ago, by a stranger, by someone whose name was lost in time, maybe even a distant ancestor. *Now when the sun says hello to the mountains, and the night says hello to the dawn.* From our spot there on the hilltop, we could see all of Fort Kent unrolled before us like a thick, warm rug, smoke rising from fireplace chimneys, yellow lights blinking on as though they were stars being born. Little supernovas. It was like looking down on a Grandma Moses painting, and yet being a part of it, too, our lives being nothing more than a couple of splotches of paint. *Je suis seul avec mes rêeves sur la montagne. Une voix me rappelle de toi. I'm alone with my dreams on the hilltop. I can still hear your voice though you're gone.*

Thomas Wolfe says you can't go home again. He meant that thought for the traveler, for the seeker who goes off into the world and then comes back to find that the place he left is irrevocably changed. But it applies to those of us who barely leave the houses where we were born and raised. It applies to all of us, for the past is lost to us forever. I put my arms around Dee Dee and hugged her tightly to me. Trooper and Lydia and Ross and Vickie finally ascended the hill one more time, their faces red with cold, their voices echoing along the ridge, full of excitement and glee.

"One more time and I'm done," said Lydia. Ross and Vickie seemed to agree. I looked over at Dee

Dee. She was almost lost beneath the thick folds of Lydia's heavy blue parka that she had borrowed for the occasion. She seemed so tiny and thin that I was hoping against hope that she'd change her mind about plowing down the hill on a sled. But I was wrong.

"It's my last chance," she whispered, and I nodded. What would I do if I were living her life? I'd want to grab at as much of it as I could. I nodded at the big sled Lydia and I had chosen with care from Quigley's Hardware.

"I go in the front, though," I said. "And you behind me. Okay?" Dee Dee nodded her enthusiasm.

"Just like when we were kids," she said. I realized she'd probably planned it that way. Ever since we were kids I'd fallen face-first into Dee Dee's plans, exactly where she'd wanted me all along.

I sat on the sled and positioned my feet on the steering bars. Dee Dee carefully climbed on behind me and wrapped her arms around my waist.

"You ready?" I asked.

"Let's go," was the reply.

"Houston!" I shouted. "We've got ignition!" And we were off, down the face of the hill, all the lights of Fort Kent glittering like winter fireflies, lights all over the St. John Valley. Dee Dee and I were flying, flying with time, flying toward our destinies like leaves in the wind. I heard her joyous cries rising up over my shoulder. I sucked in my breath as I steered us straight down the slope of Daigle Hill. But when we reached the bottom, we were traveling a bit faster than we should have been. I was rusty, I realized, at sliding down hills. I saw the edge of the trees looming ahead of us like a solid wooden fence. I'd need to cut a sharp turn, knowing it might flip us.

"Hang on tight!" I shouted over my shoulder. And then I cut the steering mechanism as sharply as I could. We veered around, a perfect cop turn, and flipped gently onto our sides. I sat up quickly and reached for Dee Dee, her hair and face covered with soft snow. She grinned up at me.

"God," she said. "It's like life, isn't it? It goes so damn fast." I stood up and brushed the snow from my pants, then reached down to help Dee Dee up. I could only imagine how much strength this outing had zapped from her, how physically painful it must have been to go sliding. And emotionally painful; it would be her last time. This was the courage she had spoken of, that night when she finally told me the truth. It takes courage to *live,* just as it does to die.

"Take my hand," I said, surprised to find that she was no longer laughing. Then I realized that she was crying. I knelt beside her in the snow, put my hand on her shoulder. I knew that she must have moments like this, lots of them, when the sadness overwhelmed her. I was thankful that she was finally letting me share in it, maybe carry some of the load for her. She was trying to be too brave, too much of the time.

"Want me to hold you?" I asked. She shook her head. I looked up to see Lydia and Vickie flying down the hill toward us, piggyback on the sled, Ross just behind them, followed by Trooper on the Flying Saucer. I caught Lydia's eye, as she and Vickie reached the bottom of the hill. I quickly made a frantic gesture, and Lydia, seeing Dee Dee slumped in my arms, got the hint.

"Hey, Troop," I heard her yell, just as Trooper arrived on the Flying Saucer. "Come look at this. You can almost see the new house out on Gagnon Road from here." She and Trooper disappeared behind some trees. Ross and Vickie, understanding the situation immediately, followed. When they were gone, I lifted Dee Dee's chin with my fingers, wiped her tears. She looked up at me like some kind of wounded animal.

"I need your help, Sammy," she said. "When the time comes, I want to be in control. I don't want to lie in a coma. I don't want Trooper to see me like that. You're a vet. You can get me pills, or whatever I need, can't you?" I was shocked. But I didn't need a lot of time to think before I answered her. I knew what I'd say, had *always known* what I'd say if Dee Dee asked me. This was one of her scenarios that I had no intention of falling blindly into.

"No," I said. "I can't, Dee Dee. Maybe with someone else. Maybe. But this is *you*. This is different."

"I'm dying, Sammy," she told me. "It's not like it's an original idea, you know. It's been going on for a long time."

"Not between you and me, it hasn't," I said. I wished I could get her to stop crying. That was almost more than I could bear. "Not between you and me," I repeated, as if it were some kind of mantra. What I was feeling surprised me greatly. I was growing angry, growing furious that she'd put me in such a spot to begin with. What the hell more did she want from me? First, she disappears from my life for almost fifteen years, without so much as a goddamn letter. Not to mention the fact that she'd run off with Bobby Langford on the very night I was going to ask her to go steady. Then she has a child whose birth I learn about *from my mother*. Next, she turns up in my life like some comet streaking across the sky, after it's been gone for a few thousand years, and I'm supposed to take her back in, supposed to adopt her son, as though that's a small thing. I'm supposed to stand by her side pretending death is okay, death is like a carnival ride, death is like sliding down a hill. I'm supposed to do all of that, on top of hanging her goddamn ABBA poster in my office. And yet, it still wasn't enough for her. How many more pounds of flesh was I supposed to give this woman who had all but disappeared from my life until she discovered she needed me?

"Please, Sammy," she said now, the tip of her nose red from the cold, or from crying, or from both. "You gotta help me die." Anger was now boiling in me. Anger was now becoming my friend, something to ease the pain of losing her.

"How dare you ask me that?" I said. I stood up, stood looking out over the valley. More snow filled the empty spaces left behind from summer and autumn. The scene before me could have been inside one of those paperweights that are filled with fake snow, the kind you shake in order to create a false storm. A counterfeit world. Hell, we could all be living inside a goddamn paperweight, for all we knew, one that God shook once in a while, when the mood hit him. "How dare you?" I asked again, and was glad to see Lydia walking toward us. She could take care of this mess. I was washing my hands of it. I, for one, had had enough.

Main Street, Fort Kent

ELEVEN

"Yes," I answered you last night;
"No," this morning, sir, I say.
Colors seen by candlelight
Will not look the same by day.
—ELIZABETH BARRETT BROWNING,
FROM ONE OF DEE DEE'S CANDLE BOXES

What can I say about anger, except that it's a warm blan-
ket that you can wrap yourself up in while outside
snow is falling on the world. I kept up with my
chores at the clinic, kept neutering and spaying, kept
patching up hernias and torn ears and broken legs.
The James Herriot of Fort Kent, Dee Dee had called me.
Autumn fell away behind us and winter moved in
with a fierce urgency. Fort Kent was settling down
on its bones for the long winter ahead, and I was determined that if I ignored Dee Dee Michaud, if I
stayed wrapped in my blanket, everything would
vanish, all the problems would drop like old leaves
and churn themselves into fertilizer for the new
spring growth. I lived with my anger and my delu-
sion, but I *lived,* damnit.

181

For almost two weeks I avoided Dee Dee Michaud to the very best of my abilities. I took detours if I had to drive beyond Bay Street. I rarely came out of the back room of my clinic, allowing paperwork to pile up on the desk in my office. I even refused to talk to Dee Dee by phone, on those occasions when she called, asking to speak to me. Lydia would nudge the receiver at my hand, urging me to take it. "Please talk to her, Sammy," my wife would plead, but those pleas fell on deaf ears. "I guess he's stepped out," Lydia would then say into the phone until, finally, she stopped covering for me altogether. "He's still being a stupid jerk, Dee Dee," she would say instead. "I'm sorry, sweetie." Yeah, well, I was sorry, too, sorry for myself. Sorry for Sam Thibodeau, who had never asked for any of this drama in the first place. "You're not mad at Dee Dee," Lydia would say. "You're just mad that she's dying." As if my troubles weren't large enough, Lydia was now suddenly one of those crazy self-help gurus we see on television, one of those twerps who are so warped and angst-laden themselves that they feel a great need to help out the rest of us poor souls. For a goodly sum, of course. "You need to come to terms with death, Sammy," Lydia said. "You're avoiding reality." I had grown tired of listening to this psychobabble and told her so. So she too withdrew, and the days reeled onward, the earth revolving around our star and taking us with it, the earth reaching the outermost apex of its orbit, so far from the sun that we would have our winter. And I, too, had revolved around Dee Dee Michaud's life until I was at the outermost reach of my own personal orbit. There was winter between us now, a coldness unlike anything I'd ever experienced before in all those years of knowing each other. Except for when I got mad at her for becoming a woman before I could become a man. Back when I used to call her *monkey* and *nitwit* and *idiot*. And that's exactly how I felt again, like an adolescent boy trying to find his way in a world of horrible truths. Truths about life and death. Finally, Dee Dee quit calling. "Tell him I'm here if he's ready to talk," she told Lydia, who, like the oft-killed messenger, delivered the message to me with a certain amount of reservation. I only nodded, pretending not to care. But I did. I cared so much that I couldn't sleep at night. In the long dark hours before morning, I'd rise and stand there at my bedroom window, trying to imagine her asleep in her own bed, over at Bay Street. Or was she up, vomiting from her illness? Suffering night sweats? Were the old memories at 204 Bay Street eating her alive, like another kind of awful cancer? I couldn't bear it. The rest of the night would find me sitting in my recliner in the living room, while Lydia slept, a glass of twelve-year-old Jack Daniel's in my hand. Booze that was three years older than the new son I would soon be raising.

Finally, Lydia brought Dee Dee's name up to me,

one morning at breakfast, and the first morning that the temperature had finally dropped below zero. *Get ready for winter,* nature was telling us, *get ready, 'cause you ain't seen nothing yet.*

"There's some terrible gossip going around town," Lydia said. "Someone started the story that Dee Dee is dying." I stared out at the bird feeder as chickadees and pine siskins and purple finches helped themselves to a breakfast of sunflower, millet, and Niger seeds. A regular breakfast buffet in the backyard. Well, Dee Dee *was* dying. And we knew it would be just a matter of time before the news swept town. That's why we had urged her to tell the truth, to everyone. It would be best.

"Trouble is," Lydia continued, "a couple of the town gossips—you know the type—well, they're telling folks that Dee Dee has AIDS." I swallowed hard at this, wondering why town gossips are allowed to ply their trade in the first place. There should have been ordinances in place, centuries ago, allowing the rest of us to gather up some nice-sized rocks and run the no-good meddlers out of town. My heart suddenly filled up with sadness that Dee Dee would have to go through this, along with everything else the cards had dealt her.

"That's a shame," I said, and Lydia seemed heartened by the fact that I was at least discussing Dee Dee Michaud again.

"When I drove her to the doctor's office yesterday,

Sam," she continued, "we met up with Florence and Alberta. Remember them? Tweedledee and Tweedledum? Even their cats are nosy." I nodded. It was true that pets are sometimes like their owners. Dogs that are beaten will often snarl and bite. Who wouldn't? But cats being nosy because they belong to gossips?

"That theory is going to take some more research before I, personally, endorse it," I said, somberly.

"When Florence met Dee Dee in the doorway," Lydia continued, "she jumped back, as if she was afraid to be near her. Then, when we stepped outside, we heard Florence tell Alberta not to touch the doorknob. It was terrible, Sam. Just terrible. Dee Dee tried to joke about it, but I could tell how deeply hurt she was." I thought about going over to Florence's and kicking her door down. Telling her off. But I didn't. I shrugged instead. I could only hope that Trooper wasn't suffering some of these slings and arrows at school.

"I thought you might want to stop by Bay Street and talk to Dee Dee," Lydia said finally, in a small, unassuming voice. I looked at her steadily as I considered this proposal.

"I got a lot of supplies to order," I mumbled. She nodded. Then she stood up and took her dishes over to put in the dishwasher. I kept my eyes on the bird feeder and remained silent.

"I'm going to take a shower," Lydia said. "And

then I'll be at Dee Dee's all day, helping her out. It's getting harder and harder for her to look after things. She's going to have to stop making candles soon. But folks are buying them up faster than she can make them, and the extra money helps out." I wanted Lydia to shut up. I wanted her to keep her news about Dee Dee and town gossips and candles to herself. And I knew what she was doing: trying to lure me back into the coils of Dee Dee's life. Well, I wasn't going to let her. Not yet, anyway.

While Lydia was showering, I went into our bedroom to finish dressing. I needed a warm shirt, a thermal undershirt, since I planned a visit to Fred Malmborg's farm to check up on a sick goat, his daughter's pet. I suspected that the goat had gotten a mouthful of something that didn't agree with it. Goats aren't fussy eaters.

"Lydia," I yelled, hoping she would hear me above the spray of the shower. "Where's my thermal underwear?" There was no response, so I went searching on my own. I found nothing of interest in my own drawer of tee shirts and socks, so I pulled open Lydia's and began rifling through it, trying hard not to spoil her stacked tiers, a thing she hated. And that's when I found the book. It was called *Dying at Home.* I sat on the side of the bed and just held it for a few moments. I could hear the water still spraying in the shower and Lydia humming some little tune. I could wait for her and ask about the book before I opened it, but I didn't. Inside I found a note, in Lydia's handwriting, outlining some pretty thoughtful steps: *(1) An hour before: cup of tea and single toast, followed by a Dramamine to ward off sickness. (2) Take a few tablets with alcohol first, then take the rest pulverized in yogurt. Must be eaten quickly! (3) Alcohol will wash pills down and dilute the bad taste.*

I closed the book and waited for my wife to reappear in the bedroom. She finally did, a towel wrapped about her, her hair piled high on her head in a makeshift ponytail. I held up the book.

"What's this?" I asked. Lydia stopped humming. At first she seemed like the proverbial deer in the headlights. Then she relaxed, as if remembering her inalienable rights as an American, as a human being.

"It's a book, Sam," she said calmly. "What does it look like?" I held it higher.

"What's it doing hiding in your dresser?" I asked.

"What were you doing *snooping* in my dresser?" Lydia asked. "You're as bad as Florence's cat." She began dressing, pulling on jeans and then a sweater.

"What's this all about, Lyddie?" I asked. She stopped lacing her shoes then, and came to sit on the bed next to me.

"Dee Dee has asked me to be there," Lydia says. "You know, when the time comes. She doesn't want to be alone, Sammy. I'm the only one she can turn to." Before I realized what I was doing, I threw the book so hard against the wall that the spine broke

187

and several pages flew out and scattered about on the floor. I felt such *jealousy* just then. That was it, no doubt about it. It was pure *jealousy*. So Lydia would be there at Dee Dee's death, would she, instead of me? Why hadn't they even bothered to tell me about this? So I asked Lydia that very question.

"Because you refuse to talk about this at all, Sammy," she answered. "And we felt you had that right, Dee Dee and I did." Oh, they did, did they? How kind of them. How goddamned kind. I wondered what other pains they had spared me, during those little clandestine meetings they were always holding in the middle of the day.

"Damn you both," I said. I put my face in my hands, as I sat there on the bed, helpless, not knowing my next move, not knowing what the hell I should or could do. I felt Lyddie's hand on my shoulder, and it seemed as if the touch of it gave me permission to cry: my wife's touch, robust and full of life, but for how long? This was the anger I felt— anger at whatever power had set this crazy world in motion—anger that we're all placed here, in this wild, insane experiment known as life. When Lydia put her arms around me I wept like a child.

"It's okay," Lydia whispered. "Cry all you can now. You'll have to be strong later, for Trooper and Dee Dee." I hated Lydia then. Hated her because she seemed so much closer to Dee Dee than I was. She had stolen Dee Dee the way Bobby Langford had stolen her. Lydia would be privy to her dying, something I was being denied. Something I had denied *myself*. I pushed her arms away from me.

"Don't," was all I said.

"Sam, I know what you're feeling," Lydia said. "That you've been left out. But Dee Dee is only trying to protect you." I wiped my eyes, then turned to look at Lydia's face, her softly arched eyebrows, the calm and quiet radiance in her eyes, the heart-shaped mouth. It was her mouth that attracted me first, that day in class. Looking down at my wife's face, my heart full of pain over losing my best friend, I realized for the first time that Lydia and Dee Dee represented the two kinds of women I had grown up loving and admiring: Lydia was Melanie, Dee Dee was Scarlett. One sensible, dependable, the very picture of good, sound logic; the other as unpredictable as a leaf in a fast-moving brook. Lydia would never have run off with Bobby Langford. After all, Lydia ran off with *me,* good old sensible, dependable Sam Thibodeau. I hated the both of them at that moment, women that they were, always certain of what a man is thinking, always *nurturing,* goddamnit, as if they're all-knowing goddesses. And a man, well, what does a *man* know about dying?

"Sammy," Lydia said just then. She put her hand back on my arm, squeezed it. "Do you want me to talk to Dee Dee?" Did *I* want *her* to talk to Dee Dee Michaud for me? Christ, I hated her! I pushed her hand away, grabbed my jacket, and stomped out to my truck.

I spent the day cruising the back roads, visiting farmer after farmer, leaning on fence after fence, discussing everything from udder infections to equine tapeworms. At 3 P.M. I stopped by Doris's Cafe, realizing that I'd had nothing to eat all day long. I hadn't even thought of food. I'd thought about Dee Dee. I would be talking to some farmer as he worked on his tractor, or I'd be lifting the foot of a horse to check the hoof, and I'd see her face, from some old memory that had taken place on the riverbank, or in homeroom at school, some drive-in movie we'd sneaked in to see, in the trunk of Ross's car. My day was filled with such memories, one after the other, until I realized I could work no longer. So I went to Doris's and ordered ployes, those buckwheat pancakes that so sustained the first Acadian settlers, and eggs, and home fried potatoes, grown right there in the St. John Valley. And sliced tomatoes. Did the Acadian pioneers have sliced tomatoes? I was just finishing my coffee when I felt someone slide into the booth next to me. It was Trooper.

"Hey," he said.

"Hey, Trooper."

"I been looking for you, Sam," he said sincerely. I

had to laugh at this. Not so long ago, *I'd* gone looking for *him*. Now, the situation was reversed. I suddenly felt like a nine-year-old boy. "I been looking everywhere," Trooper added.

"I *have* been looking," I said. Poor kid. He looked as lost as I felt. After all, what was Trooper but a miniature *man*? We were both up against Melanie and Scarlett. "What's the matter, pal?" I asked. "You want something to eat?" He shook his head. Then he looked up at me, eyes watery.

"Peter told me that my mom shouldn't be living here in Fort Kent, not with AIDS," Trooper said. His voice sounded smaller, more distant than ever. "Peter told me that his mom and Mrs. Humphrey said they wouldn't touch a candle if it came from Bay Street." Peter's mom and Mrs. Humphrey. *Florence and Alberta. Tweedledee and Tweedledum.* I looked down at his little shoulders, tiny for a kid approaching his tenth birthday. With time, he would fill out. The years would make him tall and strong. He had his father's long legs, his father's good looks. But he had Dee Dee's heart.

"You know what I think?" I said finally.

"What?" asked Trooper, and he looked up at me with such trust just then. *This is what it means to be a parent,* I told myself. *So be careful.*

"I think Peter doesn't sound like a very good friend."

"Me, too," said Trooper.

"And I think his mom and Mrs. Humphrey aren't very nice people."

"Yeah," said Trooper, and he seemed relieved that an adult had verified what he'd been feeling, too.

"You got other friends," I said. "You don't need someone like Peter. You don't need mean people." Trooper nodded. Being a good parent, I'd decided, meant I couldn't add that Peter's mother and Mrs. Humphrey had closets stuffed full of their own skeletons. Closets full of skeletons are what motivate most gossips in the first place. Doris put a glass of chocolate milk down in front of Trooper.

"Thanks," he said, and took a sip.

"You know, Troop," I said, "we men have got to stick together. Lydia and your mom, they're so busy seeing that everything is done just right that they've sort of forgotten about us." He nodded.

"I don't want her to die, Sam," he said. I could barely hear his words. I watched as he ran his index finger around the rim of his glass.

"Me either, Troop," I said. "Me either." He stood up, pushed the half-full glass of milk back across the counter, then searched in his pockets for his gloves.

"I gotta go home," he said. "I gotta feed Lancelot." He started toward the door, then changed his mind. He came back over to the booth, slid into it, and then wrapped his arms around me. I hugged back, then patted him on the head.

"Us guys need to look out for each other, Sam," Trooper said.

I was just turning into the drive at the clinic when Sue Gauvin roared in, the horn blasting on her Cherokee Laredo. She jumped out, her face torn with agony as she struggled for words. I bounded out of my truck and raced over to her.

"Sue, what's the matter?" I asked. She had begun to sob, and now she simply pointed to the back of the truck. That's when I saw her husband, Paul, crawling out of the back of the Laredo with something in his arms—Cody, the five-year-old collie that I'd been doctoring for as long as I'd been in practice in northern Maine.

"A deliveryman forgot to close our gate," Paul said as he looked down at the limp dog in his arms. "A car struck him, Sam." Both he and Sue were frantic.

"Get him into the back room," I said. "Hurry." I quickly opened the clinic's door and stepped back as Paul carried the dog into the examining room.

I could tell by Cody's eyes that the situation didn't look good. His pupils were nonresponsive to my penlight, and his gums were very pale.

"I need to take an X ray," I said to Paul. "I'll be just a few minutes."

When Paul left the room, I carried Cody over to the X-ray table and placed him gently on it. I put a film in the tray, and then estimated that the dog's back was about 15 centimeters thick. I checked the chart I kept hanging on the wall—this would tell me what measurement of radiation to use—and set the dials on the X-ray machine accordingly. Then I pressed the foot pedal to shoot the picture. Next I took the tray into the tiny darkroom I'd had built for this purpose, removed the film, and fed it into the automatic processor. In less than a minute I was studying Cody's X ray. It revealed what I feared most: a crushed lumbar vertebra, which meant that the damage to the spinal cord running through that bone was irreparable. And the abdominal cavity was full of fluid, caused by a probable ruptured spleen. I went out to tell Paul Gauvin the bad news.

"Is there anything we can do?" he asked.

"If you want, we can try to save him," I said. But I knew Paul could tell by the tone of my voice that I was not hopeful.

"Will he recover fully?" he wanted to know.

"The first problem is to get the bleeding stopped," I said, "but I seriously doubt that Cody will ever walk again." I saw Paul's eyes tear instantly. He said nothing for a few seconds. Then he asked what a lot of my clients ask.

"What would you do if it were *your* dog?"

There it is, the sixty-four-thousand-dollar question. When a client puts it to me that way, they want me to offer them my expertise. But I don't tell them the full story, of how many times I've seen a dog or cat suffer for days before finally giving up. I don't tell them of the pain in an animal's eyes. *Can't you stop this?* the eyes ask. *Can't you do something?* But I'm helpless if the owner isn't ready to let the animal go. It's a rock and a hard place, no doubt about it. And Cody's outlook was about as bad as it gets. So, I told Paul Gauvin the truth. Maybe Cody would live. Maybe. But there would be excruciating pain during the period of time that he recuperated. If he ended up paralyzed, and I was quite certain that he would, his bladder and colon wouldn't function normally. This would mean that someone would need to express the bladder manually, four or five times a day. Laxatives and enemas would be required, with a nonfunctioning colon. And, of course, the animal would need to be put on a special diet. Some pet owners still opt to keep the animal alive at this point. If it survives the injury, they buy it a specially ordered cart with wheels, so that the animal can still pull itself about. And some of those pets do well under those circumstances. A rock and a damned hard place. But Paul had asked me a very specific question. What would I, personally, do if it were *my* dog? So I answered him honestly.

"I think I'd let Cody go," I said. Paul nodded. He seemed relieved that I'd taken this heavy decision from off his shoulders. Sometimes, who makes the final decision is what this difficult time is all about. And that was part of my job, too.

"We need to go home and talk to Ashley," Paul said, and I nodded. Everything takes time.

After the Gauvins left, I injected Cody with 3 ccs of Oxymorphone. It wouldn't take the pain away, but it would dull it some. A half hour later, the bell over the front door of the clinic rang out. The Gauvins were back. They had talked to their daughter, explained the circumstances to her as best they could. They didn't want Cody to suffer any longer. Now, the three of them had come to say a quick good-bye. I left them alone in the back, knowing they'd want some privacy. After a few minutes, they emerged with tear-filled eyes. I could tell that the parents were being strong for the young girl. I nodded to Sue as she opened the front door, her arm around her daughter. Paul hung back.

"We're gonna go on home," he said. "It's better for Ashley." I agreed. It would be better. They'd said their good-bye to Cody. Rituals come in all shapes and sizes. Some people insist on being there at the last moment for their pets, stroking them, whispering words of comfort until the end. Others walk away. Either way is tough. Each person is different in handling grief. And yes, there are some people who really don't care much at all if their pet dies. I've had people with a sizable bank account tell me to put their animal down because of a simple leg break. The Gauvins went home.

Alone, in the back room, I sat looking into Cody's

eyes, stroking the dog's head. I didn't want to waste any more time, cause him any more pain than was necessary. I wished Lydia was there to help out, spiritually if not physically. I shaved a spot on Cody's front leg, small and white, like a field of freshly fallen snow.

"There, Cody," I said, speaking for the Gauvins, knowing what they would say to their beloved dog if they had been there. "It's okay, boy. It's gonna be okay. Good dog. That's a good dog." As I filled a needle with pentobarbital, I continued to speak to him, my voice steady and soothing. Cody couldn't lift his tail, could probably no longer even feel it there. But his front paw moved, slightly, as he attempted one final communication. Still talking calmly, I inserted the needle into the narrow vein and injected the poison. A few seconds passed. There was a sudden foul smell, one that I had expected as Cody's bowels emptied on the table. It was over.

I sat there for a long time, staring down at the dead dog before me, tears streaming down my face in an uncontrollable flow. Dee Dee had asked me to help her die, thinking, I suppose, that because I was a vet I would have the means to do so. I could slip her some pills. Maybe give her a needle full of poison. But if I gave her enough pills to kill herself, I would surely lose my license to practice, not to mention possible jail time. And while I could fill a needle with enough pentobarbital to put an animal to sleep forever, if I gave Dee Dee that same needle, she would fall asleep from the first gushes of it into her veins before she could inject enough of it to kill herself. Vets who commit suicide hook themselves up to a catheter, so that after they fall asleep, the poison will still drip down until enough of it is in their system. If I was going to help her, I had to find a way that would do the job without implicating me in any way. After all, I still had a life to live. And a small boy to raise.

I phoned Ross. He sounded sleepy, but I didn't care that I might have awakened him from his after-dinner nap. This was more important.

"Do you still have that doctor friend of yours in Quebec City?" I asked him. "The one you told me about?" Ross paused a moment.

"Yeah," he said finally. He had told me how this friend of his, this doctor, had helped terminal patients die when the pain was too great and all hope was gone. This doctor did it in secret, Ross said, because it's still against the law. I suspected doctors all over the world were doing such things in secret: We're a society that still doesn't know how to die. Some of us don't know how to *live*. "What about him?"

"I need about two hundred milligrams of morphine," I said. "It comes in fifteen-milligram tablets, so I'll need fourteen of them." I heard Ross's sudden intake of breath. And then he exhaled.

"Dee Dee?" he asked.

"Yeah, Dee Dee," I told him. "Can you drive to Quebec and get them?" Ross said nothing for a long time. I wondered if he, too, was remembering that wild February weekend in Quebec City, the one Dee Dee had said was her best memory of the old times, when a bunch of us from our senior class had driven up for the Winter Carnival. This was the night Dee Dee had danced about the bar of the Château Frontenac, silver streamers cascading behind her. Dawn had found us bleary-eyed at a window overlooking the St. Lawrence, in a room we could afford only because we'd all pooled our money. As the sun rose over the river, I remember feeling transcended at just the sight of it, golden and eternal. Most of us in that room were descended from those first settlers who had made their way up that very river to found Quebec. We were blood of their blood. Streets in the old part of the city—*la ville vieille*—were named with our family surnames. Our ancestral grandfather, Abraham Martin, had been ship's pilot for Champlain; the Plains of Abraham, not far away from our motel room, where Abraham's cattle had grazed, had been named in his honor. In his will, Champlain had bequeathed to Abraham Martin *a suit of clothes*. I felt a wonderful sense of permanency that night, staring out that window, Ross, Dee Dee, and I the only ones left awake to pass around a bottle of good French wine. I was immortal that night. So was Dee

Dee, and Ross. I was certain we'd all live forever. What a young fool I'd been.

"I can get them," Ross said finally. I could hear a sad, bleak acceptance in his voice. Maybe we all thought something would happen to change the inevitable. Some kind of sweet miracle, like winning the lottery. Everyone but Dee Dee, who had known the truth all along. Well, the inevitable was now knocking on our front doors.

I hung up the phone from talking with Ross and reached for my coat. I met Lydia at the door. She was stomping snow from her boots, taking off her coat and scarf. She smiled at me. *How did I ever find you?* I wondered. *In this great big world, how did I ever get so lucky?* She gave me a *what's up?* look.

"I'm going over to Bay Street," I said. "To talk to Dee Dee." Lydia looked at me, deciphering, I suppose.

"Here," she said, and handed me her scarf. "It's cold out."

I walked to 204 Bay Street, wanting to feel the cold in my bones, in the very marrow of my soul; wanting to breathe in the crisp air, the twinkling night sky over Canada, the eternal stars, the old comfortable streets of Fort Kent, Maine. I wanted my thoughts to get themselves in order, to make sure I knew what was what. *We help our pets leave this world with as much dignity as possible,* I told myself. *We help our pets die when the time is right.*

Dee Dee answered her front door, looking sleepy, like a little girl who's been waiting up half the night for Santa Claus. Some Santa Claus I was. I heard the snow on her porch crunch beneath my boots as I leaned on one foot and then the other, hands in my jacket pockets, my breath escaping in gray clouds.

"Sammy?" she said. "Is something wrong? Did Lyddie get home okay?" She was dying, and yet she wanted to know if Lydia was okay. I stepped in past her and shut the door. I didn't want her to catch cold. Her immune system was already weakened. Our job now would be to keep her alive and in our lives for as long as we could. I looked up the stairs, saw light hovering beneath Trooper's bedroom door. The room where my future son was probably getting ready for bed. He'd come to my rescue earlier in the day. I would do the same for him, whenever life dealt him a bad hand. I'd be there. And I would be there for his mother, too, for my old friend, my compadre. The first woman I'd ever loved. Because first loves die hard. They die damn hard.

"I'll help you," I told Dee Dee. What did I think she'd do? Skip some light fantastic out of town? What did I think she'd say? *Hey, Sammy, it's all been a big joke. Ain't life a hoot?* "I'll help you," I said again. And those were the only words that were necessary between us. Dee Dee didn't speak at all. She just put her frail arms up around my neck, and lay her head on my shoulder. I put my own arms about her waist, my chin on the top of her head. It was as if we were dancing, the way we had done at all those school dances, with me awkward and certain I'd be stepping on her toes before the night was over. But I didn't step on her toes on this night. Instead, I held her close to me, breathed in the sweet, herbal smell of her hair, and tried to imagine what my life was going to be like when she was no longer in it.

Church at Baker Brook, New Brunswick

TWELVE

But when night is on the hills,
And the great Voices roll in from the sea,
By starlight and by candlelight and by dreamlight
She comes to me.
—HERBERT TRENCH (1865–1923),
FROM ONE OF DEE DEE'S CANDLE BOXES

Snow covered the St. John Valley and winter fully claimed the land as its own. Red and orange leaves were now just memories as deciduous trees stood stark and bare along the river and on the mountain ridges. The warblers, too, and other birds that had flown south for the winter, were memories, as were the yellow daisies and orange hawkweed that had grown in all the pastures around the valley. The St. John River had not yet frozen over, but ice had formed on water spots in some of the bare potato fields and on the ponds. Now those fields were dotted with the hardiest of skaters. The less hardy, who chose the comfort of the town's rink, would be rewarded with hot chocolate and smoother ice. The birds of winter were busy searching out the last of the summer berries, shaking the branches of the mountain ash as they did so. Dee Dee's business didn't fail after news of her illness swept around town, no thanks to Florence and Alberta. On the contrary, Fort Kenters were eager to buy up every candle Dee Dee made. And then Candles on Bay Street simply grew too demanding. An assembly line might turn out enough candles but Dee Dee couldn't do it by hand any longer, not with her illness pulling her down, sapping her energy. Finally, she had to close down shop. All we could hope for then, with Thanksgiving upon us, was that she would make it until Christmas. Dee Dee was eternally philosophical about the whole thing. "I don't want to die at Christmas, or New Year's," she told us. "That will spoil all of Trooper's holidays for the rest of his life. He'll be reminded of *me,* when he should be having fun." We never spoke the words, but we all knew that she would soon choose a time. Her greatest fear all along had been of losing control. Dee Dee would choose a time when she still had the strength to go through with it.

Thanksgiving came and went, with Lydia and me bringing trays of food to Dee Dee's house. Lydia set the big table in the dining room, using the linen Dee Dee's own mother had used, back in those days when everyone was still safe and sound on Bay Street. I lit Dee Dee's own handmade tapered candles. Trooper even wore a suit, something none of us adults had asked him to do, or had even *cared* that he do. But we all sensed that he was feeling some need to formalize each gathering, to make it important. It was, after all, the last Thanksgiving he'd be spending with his mother.

People were probably still eating turkey sandwiches in most of the houses in Fort Kent when Dee Dee decided that the time was at hand. She was getting ready. The dreaded moment in our lives was hovering nearby. She had grown weaker by the day, and the pain had grown stronger. Pills were no longer helping. "I'm not gonna make it to Christmas," Dee Dee finally told us, and our worst fears were realized. Now we would have to meet the next set of fears with bravery, and that would be when she decided upon an actual day. It was already the last week of November. The year was running out and another one was upon us. A brand-new year that Dee Dee Michaud would not live to see. Lydia had already packed her suitcase and gone to stay permanently at 204 Bay Street. Now we were waiting, even though we pretended we weren't. We were waiting for the next and last move of the game.

Even when you're expecting it, you're not ready for death. On the first day of December, a cold and brightly sunny day, I decided to drive to Caribou, sixty miles away, to pick up a small Jonsred chain saw for cutting my winter firewood. On the spur of the moment—at least I told myself it was the spur of the moment—I stopped in for a morning cup of coffee with my wife. I wasn't having a great time sleeping without Lydia at my side, but I knew Dee Dee needed her more. And while I was still trying my best to accept the circumstances of Dee Dee's impending death, acceptance was not coming easily. The idea still seemed too random and too unfair for my tastes. But, for Dee Dee's sake, I was putting on the best performance I could.

Lydia had just placed a cup of fresh coffee in front of me when Dee Dee dropped the bomb, so to speak. She'd chosen a day. She was ready to die. I felt my insides churn a bit and then go numb.

"Next Monday," Dee Dee said. "December 7. It's perfect because it's past Thanksgiving, and yet it's still three weeks from Christmas. It's *Pearl Harbor Day*, for crying out loud. What's to spoil?" I took a drink of my coffee and found I could taste nothing. It may as well have been ink. I looked over at Dee Dee and tried to smile. She was still thinking of Trooper, of not spoiling a holiday for him. But it had been obvious for some time to those of us who loved her that she wouldn't make it until Christmas. She was feverish most of the time, and her night sweats were now so frequent that Lydia was getting up several times a night to change the bedsheets. The severe pain in her stomach was worse. She had little appetite for food, and when she finally did eat something, she usually experienced nausea, sometimes followed by vomiting. We had already discussed a plan—the three of us, along with Ross and Vickie—for when the time came. Funny, but Dee Dee, Ross, and I used to plan assaults on the teachers' room. All-night keg parties. Now we were planning Dee Dee's death.

"Have you told Trooper yet?" I asked, wondering what he would do, now that the time had finally arrived. Lydia shook her head.

"Dee Dee's telling him tonight," she answered softly. Then she tried to fill my coffee cup, but I stopped her. What good would more coffee do, when I couldn't even taste what I had?

"I'll call Dr. LaPorte today and tell him I'm ready to be hospitalized," said Dee Dee. She seemed even more tired than usual. But lately I had been noticing something else in her, some quiet determination that kept pushing her onward. I wondered if that was nature's way of preparing us, maybe shooting some endorphins into our systems at times like this, to soften the blow. "Dr. LaPorte has wanted me to check into the hospital for a couple weeks now," Dee Dee continued. "I'll tell him that I'm gonna admit myself on December 8." As if desensitized by what was happening, Lydia and I nodded like trained seals. We knew the rest of the plan. Ross and Vickie would spread the word to Dee Dee's friends that she'd be going into the hospital. It was time to say goodbye. They could do so next Monday evening—now that Dee Dee had chosen a day—by attending a small gathering that we would hold here at 204 Bay Street. Friends could drop by and visit with Dee Dee one more time. Then, after they'd all gone, Dee Dee would say goodbye to Trooper. Once that unimaginable episode was over, Ross and Vickie would take Trooper over to his bedroom at our house. It would be difficult for him, for everyone. But this is death. There *is* no easy way, and Dee Dee had done her best to help Trooper make the transition to his new life. Then, when Ross and Vickie left with Trooper, I would wait in the kitchen while Lydia gave Dee Dee a sponge bath and helped her into her nightgown. Dee Dee wanted to die in the parlor, with all her candles lit. So Lydia and I would make up the sofa bed for her there. We would stay with her, until she instructed us that the time had come. That would be our cue to leave the room while she took the pills, just as Lydia's instruction list said to. That way, if Lydia and I were questioned as to whether we saw Dee Dee take any pills, we could truthfully say no. *Knowing* and *assisting* are two different things. Then, when Dee Dee was gone—I could barely imagine this part of the plan—Lydia and I would walk home. Lydia would "find" Dee Dee the next day. No one knew anything about her plans, or so we would say. Like everyone else, we thought she was going into the hospital. That's what we would tell the police, or anyone who asked. Where did she get the pills? Probably from someone back in Wyoming. With

Dee Dee, who's to know? We had gone over it so many times that it no longer seemed real. It seemed like a Hollywood script that could be changed at the last minute. But hope was still alive in us then.

"Can you call Ross?" Dee Dee asked weakly. "Can he go for the pills?" I nodded. Then I stood up, leaving my cup of coffee on the table.

"Listen, you two schemers," I said, "I gotta get to Caribou before the day is over."

I went out to my truck, backed it out of the yard, and pointed it straight down Route 1, the beginning of the long journey to Key West, Florida—two thousand, one hundred and nine miles long—a trip only the bravest tourist made over summer vacation. There had even been a documentary done on this historic route, when the movie star Van Heflin turned up in town, wearing a long fur coat and a fur hat, with a camera crew in tow. Fort Kent had buzzed with excitement, until, filming over, the star, and the cameras, and the fur hat disappeared as quickly as they had come. I hadn't planned to take Route 1 when I got up that morning. It was a spontaneous act but now it seemed like a fine idea. I would follow the St. John River all the way to Van Buren, before swinging south toward Caribou. It was longer this way, true, but there was something medicinal in treading along beside that old river, in watching it unfurl cold and blue as an ancient dream, for mile after mile. Our ancestors had used that river as a highway, and now, all these generations later, I had come back to it for comfort. I had come to it for sympathy and consolation, knowing it would be there.

I had not been on Route 1 for some time, so I hummed as I drove along, my eye tracing the corkscrews of smoke rising up from chimneys on the Canadian side of the river, warm and cozy homes in Baker Brook, Edmundston, St.-Jacques, Rivière-Verte. Church steeples grew on the horizon of each little town, sharp and gray against the sky. A cold, bitter mist hovered above the open water and floated up the riverbank, like ghosts of those first settlers. *The river is sure to freeze over soon,* I thought. Then I went back to the business that lay ahead, in Caribou, as though the task itself were a kind of mantra: *I need to buy a chain saw, I need to buy a chain saw, I need to buy a chain saw,* I told myself again and again. I was almost to Van Buren when I pulled over into a side road and cried for a full twenty minutes. Loud, uncontrollable sobs that I was thankful no one I knew and loved would hear. This was my private moment. This was my own soliloquy. Then, ready for the next act, I pulled back out onto Route 1 and drove on.

Two days later, Ross gassed his car up at the Irving station, next to Bee Jay's Tavern, checked the oil and the tires, then bought himself a bean burrito.

Taco Bell had just ensconced itself inside the Irving station, competition for McDonald's, and now Ross was experiencing his first Mexican meal in Fort Kent.

"Bring that to Bee Jay's with you," I told him. "We need to talk."

Lise put a beer in front of each of us and then disappeared into the back to do a chore. I was relieved because I wanted to talk to Ross privately. Most of the others who were at Bee Jay's that early in the day were over at the pool table, involved in a heated game. I recognized Andrew Jackson, from nearby Allagash, one of the best players for miles around. I hoped his opponent—who was no one I knew from town—hadn't bet much money. At the other end of the bar, a couple guys were watching TV. Barry Ouellette, a local river guide, was playing a game of cribbage with Mike Hafford. Nobody was interested in Ross and me.

"How you gonna get the pills across the border?" I asked as he took the last bites of the burrito. "You gonna just drive them across?" Ross nodded.

"I know that's taking a chance," he said, "but I don't think Stephen Renaud or Chuck Delorme is working tonight." He was referring to the customs officials who would search a man's belly button for smuggled lint, guys who got a kick out of making folks they'd known all their lives get out of their cars so that they could search behind hubcaps, under floor mats. Guys who yearned for some real *big*

213

smuggling deals. Guys who had watched too much *Miami Vice.*

"You're not sure?" I asked him as I cracked a peanut. Most folks who frequented Bee Jay's tossed their peanut husks on the floor—it was the norm—but I still couldn't bring myself to do it, as if maybe my mom would appear and say, "You pick that up right this minute, mister!"

"Naw," Ross replied. "I'm not sure. And I didn't dare ask anyone. You know, in case they put two and two together later on." I thought about Ross's answer. He was right. We couldn't go around inquiring about the schedules of customs officials suddenly. This was too little a town for stuff like that. And Ross was the last guy who should ask such questions. He still looked too much like that stoned guy on the old TV show *Taxi,* the aging hippie. It was just too big a chance to take. I ate a few more peanuts and tried to think. Even if a so-called *normal* customs official was on duty—someone who wouldn't go to ridiculous measures to search the people who live and travel on each side of the border—how could we be sure that *that* official would be on duty when Ross returned from Quebec City and was ready to cross? What if he or she took a five-minute coffee break at the wrong time, at least for us? And, usually, there were two officials on duty at all times. That second person could easily be Stephen Renaud or Chuck Delorme.

There was no way we could guarantee who the official would be when Ross Cloutier finally drove up to the booth to be asked, "Anything to declare?" Well, that would be a statement for the papers, wouldn't it? What could Ross say? *Well, actually, I got two hundred milligrams of morphine in my pocket here. But don't worry. I'm just helping a friend commit suicide.*

I leaned back and looked up at the business tiles above my head, over the barstools where we sat. It was always fun to read a different part of the ceiling at Bee Jay's, depending on where you were sitting. *Shear Perfection Beauty Salon: Connie, Tracey, Doreen & Stacey, Stylists. Fort Kent Rotary Club, Established 1952. Country Cottage, Books & Gifts, Giselle Charette, Owner.* I smiled. We had all gone to school with Giselle, who was well read and well traveled, and yet she chose to open a business right here in Fort Kent. Ross interrupted my reverie.

"So what are we gonna do?" he asked. "My doctor friend knows I'm coming. As a matter of fact," he added, looking at his watch. "I should have left a half hour ago. I'm meeting him at the bar in the Château Frontenac." I nodded, but said nothing. It was symbolic, of course, that Ross would set the meeting up at the Château Frontenac, memory bank for our big Quebec Winter Carnival night. There would probably still be ghosts of our younger selves in there, Dee Dee dancing on the bar, Ross and I swilling wine.

215

"Here's what we do," I said finally. "Just to be safe. The river is still running clear. There's gonna be a lot of slush in it, true, but I can get my canoe and motor down the bank. I'll meet you over on the Canadian side, just behind the church at Baker Brook." Ross thought about this.

"Man, oh, man," said Ross. "Ain't that dangerous?"

"*Isn't* that dangerous," I corrected him. "You're a schoolteacher, Ross, for Chrissakes. You oughta watch what you say."

"Just for the record, dude," said Ross, "I teach history. Now, what if you drown? Can I have that new chain saw?"

"I won't drown," I told him. He was joking, of course, but I knew he was worried. "Just call me when you get to Clair. I'll need less than an hour to get my canoe and motor into the water, and then over to the bank behind the church."

Ross leaned back and read a few tiles on the ceiling, trying, I suppose, to collect himself for the emotional drive that lay ahead.

" 'Congratulations, Sammy Pelletier, Winner of the 1983 Philadelphia Marathon,' " he read, eyeing the tile just above our heads. Ross Cloutier would have eight hours in which to think heavily about what we were doing.

"Local boy does good," I said. Then, "You gonna be okay?"

"Hey," Ross said, and pointed at the tile. "Remember how Sammy was always running to catch the school bus?" I nodded.

"Early training," I said. Could the talk get any smaller? Finally, Ross tossed the rest of his Pepsi back and stood up.

"Time to head out for Dodge City, cowboy," he said. I reached over and gave his hand a quick shake. I could see tears glistening in his eyes.

"Take care of yourself, buddy," I told him. "I wouldn't want to lose you, too."

Ross pulled out of Bee Jay's, a Styrofoam cup of coffee in his hand. I stood watching as his car took a right turn and then disappeared across the international bridge. Then I went back to my place and spent an hour making sure everything was fine with my canoe and motor. I filled the gas tank and left the canoe there, where I could quickly transport it later, when I got the call from Ross. Then I phoned Lydia over at Dee Dee's house and told her what was up. Ross was on his way to Quebec City. He would phone me around nine o'clock and I would meet him, by canoe, over on the Canadian side. That way, I could bring the pills back myself and no customs official would confiscate them.

"Isn't that dangerous, Sam?" Lydia asked. I assured her as best I could. After all, modern-day smugglers had used the river at all times of the year to smuggle cartons of cigarettes over to Canada, before Canada lifted its exorbitant cigarette tax. I would use the river, and I realized now why I had taken Route 1, on my Caribou trip two days earlier. I could still see the steeple of the church at Baker Brook, rising up like a black pencil on the horizon. This plan must have started cooking in the back of my mind right then.

"It's the only way to be totally safe," I told Lydia.

It was a long and somber day, the third of December was. I suppose that I will probably have grandkids one day. And if they should ever crawl up onto my lap, tug at my ear, and say, "Grandpa, what was the longest day of your life?" I'll pick *that* day, December 3, 1997, D-Day. And D, of course, would be for Dee Dee. For one thing, I couldn't seem to shake the blues. No matter how hard I tried to concentrate on other things, I *could not* do it. I even imagined that I would rush over to 204 Bay Street and talk Dee Dee out of this film noir we were all acting in. But then I'd talk to myself for a minute, calm myself down. *Just what are her alternatives?* I'd ask myself. I wasn't blind. I could see how fast she was deteriorating. And the truth is that I'd probably do the same thing if I were in her shoes. It was that knowledge, sad as it was, that held me fast to my promise to help her.

While I waited, I did the awful homework of reading up on how to die: how to take the pills; how alcohol doubles the toxicity; how speed is required—not just internally to achieve rapid death; ingestion must be quick, too, or patients could fall asleep while taking the pills. I read on and on, the clock ticking like a damn bomb over my shoulder.

At suppertime, I took a break and went to Claude's Restaurant and had a salad. It was all I could think of eating, something light so that my stomach wouldn't rebel. Then I went back to the office. Every creak in the house caused me to jump. Every passing car. Every distant voice on the street outside. A phone *not ringing* is a loud, annoying thing. Then, just before nine o'clock, I heard footsteps approaching the front door of the clinic. I assumed that Lydia was coming home to check up on how things were going. But I looked up to see Dee Dee Michaud slip inside the door. She was all bundled up in black clothing: black parka, black woolen pants, black hat and gloves.

"What the hell?" I heard myself ask.

"Lydia is with Trooper," Dee Dee said. "And you're not to be mad at her. She had no choice. I want to go with you, Sammy." I didn't know what to say. Of all the people I might have expected to come through that door, asking to go with me—from Captain Kangaroo to Barbara Walters—Dee Dee was last on the list. She was too weak, too sick for such a cold and icy trip across a black and dangerously high river.

"You're crazy," I said. I picked up the phone to call

Lydia. "This is insane," I added as she reached over and covered my hand with hers. I looked up at her, even though it hurt, even though I'd stopped seeing the old Dee Dee in her ravaged face weeks and weeks ago. But in her *eyes,* well, that was a different story. In her eyes I could still see that old fire. I could see the Dee Dee who had painted her valentine black, because everyone else in the third grade had painted theirs red; the Dee Dee who had crawled across some jerk's yard to rescue his abused dog; the Dee Dee who could trounce all the guys in a quarter-mile car race; the Dee Dee who ran away with Bobby Langford because life was such a hoot. What would I myself want to do if I were dying? I'd want to fill my hands full of everything I could pick up, all I could carry of life. I'd want every second, every stone unturned, every gauntlet taken up, until I no longer had the strength to even *think* of gauntlets. That's what I would want, and it's what Dee Dee wanted, too.

I said nothing as I put the phone back on its cradle. Dee Dee settled down in my guest chair, made herself as comfortable as possible. As we waited, the silence grew between us like a deep black lake. Finally, the phone rang. I grabbed it up in its second bleat. It was Ross. He was leaving Clair to drive down to the church at Baker Brook.

"Now it's *your* turn to be careful," I heard Ross say,

his voice tiny and sounding too far away to be just across the border. "I don't want to lose you, either, man." I hung up the phone and stood.

"Let's go, Amelia Earhart," I said to Dee Dee. I helped her out to the truck and situated her as comfortably as I could on the passenger side. Then, I backed the truck up to the garage and loaded the canoe into the body, trying my best not to be seen by anyone, especially by a Florence or an Alberta. *Tweedledee and Tweedledum.*

When we arrived at the road leading down to the river—the one where the plow turns around—I smiled to see that it had, indeed, been scraped clean of snow. That would save me some knee-high wading, all the while balancing a canoe on my head. Dee Dee followed me, close behind.

"Take each step carefully," I whispered to her. "You don't want to fall." With my pole I broke the shore ice, which had formed about a half inch thick. I then slipped the canoe partway into the water, and positioned Dee Dee in the bow. I covered her with a thick blanket, then eased the canoe out so that I could climb into the stern. I pushed us off with the pole, out into the black waters, and was surprised at how soon I was unable to reach bottom. That's how much the river had grown, thanks to all the fallen snow. I let us drift downstream, away from any houses, before I started the motor. Then, knowing the river was too high for any dangerous rocks, I gave the engine a shot of power and we motored nicely downstream.

It was a spectacular night, what with a waxing gibbous moon and stars the size of teacups. I kept my eyes protectively on Dee Dee's little silhouette, just ahead of me in the canoe. Despite the reason for this trip, the night was alive with excitement. I could feel an electricity building in me that I thought had gone away, would never be back again, the electricity of doing something outside the rules, a passion I suspected that Steve Renaud and Chuck Delorme would never experience during the long careers they would have wearing those well-pressed suits.

Dee Dee made no noise in front of me, but I could see her head leaning back to look up at the magnificent stars overhead, to keep a watch on the occasional passing house on the riverbank, its warm lights looking out at us like watchful yellow eyes. Within fifteen minutes the church at Baker Brook, New Brunswick, swept into view, its beautiful, ornate steeple outlined under the glorious moon. I cut the engine and then paddled us quickly to shore. I carefully pulled the canoe up onto the bank, gently as I could, what with Dee Dee still in the bow.

"Wait here," I told her. "I'll climb the bank. Ross should be parked up in the churchyard." But before I could leave, Dee Dee reached up a hand to stop me.

"Do you want to be there?" she asked. I felt an awkward moment pass just then. I wanted no more talk of death, not on that night, a night when we were back on the old river, beneath a show-off moon. A night of pure adrenaline.

"Do I want to be where?" I asked, and foolishly, for I knew exactly what she meant.

"When I take the pills," Dee Dee answered. "You know, Sammy. When I die. Do you want to be there? The only reason I didn't ask you, the only reason I asked Lyddie is, well, what could you say? I didn't want to put you in a tough situation, Sammy." In the moonlight I could almost make out her eyes, dark sparkling eyes.

"Dee Dee Michaud," I said, "when have you NOT put me in a tough situation?"

I left her there in the canoe, and made my way to the bottom of the hill. I slowly climbed the steep bank. When I reached the top, I could see Ross's car, waiting for me in the church's parking lot. I would be getting pills from Ross, pills that would eventually kill the most extraordinary person I had ever known. I tried not to think of this as I fought my way through a gaggle of frozen chokecherry and hazelnut bushes, just at the crest of the hill. When I finally got through the tangles, I paused. Suddenly, I heard Dee Dee yelling, from the canoe down below.

"Hey, Fernando!" she shouted up at me, her voice

resounding along the black riverbank, rolling up the hill to find me. As if her words had been in echo, from all those long years ago, and were just now returning. "Hey, Fernando!" Dee Dee shouted again. "Can you hear the guns, baby?"

The procession

THIRTEEN

My candle burns at both ends;
It will not last the night;
But, ah, my foes, and, oh, my friends—
It gives a lovely light.
—EDNA ST. VINCENT MILLAY,
FROM ONE OF DEE DEE'S CANDLE BOXES

On the morning of December 7, I rose just before dawn and went down to the kitchen to make a pot of coffee. I hadn't been able to sleep much, reaching out now and then in the night to touch the cold spot that should have been warm from Lydia's body. Poor Lydia. How could she have known, when she launched out on a career in veterinary medicine, that she would end up in Fort Kent, Maine, ministering to her husband's first true love? That she would aid in the taking of a human life? As daylight inched its way in over Fort Kent, I leaned my forehead against the cold window. In the backyard the mountain ash berries were still clinging to the branches, icy red beneath the crush of winter. Last year, a rare flock of Bohemian waxwings, Arctic birds that had come "south" to Fort Kent for the winter, had bent the branches on the ash as they clung to them, delighted to have found such a hearty breakfast. It was a rare treat. Lydia, the birder in the family, had been elated for weeks, calling other birders to tell them the news. Funny, but that's how I felt about Dee Dee Michaud moving home, something rare coming, however fleetingly, into our midst.

I turned and looked down the hill, out over the St. John Valley. I didn't know how it was possible the world could spin on, on this of all days, but it did. I saw Armory "Arms" Nadeau unroll the awning at his furniture store. There was a time, long before Radio Shack came to town, and long before CDs, that Dee Dee and I bought our 45s at Nadeau's House of Furniture. As I watched, the streets of town began to fill up as more and more folks went off to work early. And then a school bus or two inched by. The international bridge glistened with ice. Occasionally, a truck made the crossing from Canada to the United States, its tiny headlights two yellow dots among all that white, loggers no doubt. Woodsmen on their way to work. I imagined them pulling in to Rock's Diner, right next to Bee Jay's Tavern, for their morning coffee, and scrambled eggs, and cigarettes, before heading off to a long week of hard work for one of the large lumber companies. Rock's opened before the birds got up. I remembered those mornings, so many years ago, when Dee Dee, Ross, and I had partied all night long, only to find ourselves on the red Naugahyde stools at Rock's, pretending in front of Mrs. Robichaud, the cashier, that we'd just gotten up, and then making individual plans as to how we could sneak into our parents' houses without them catching us. That was half our lifetimes ago. And yet, in the great wash of time, it was not even a second. I stood quietly, looking down on the little town where we three had been born, a town that had shaped us, a town we loved. I tried desperately to form one single thought in my mind so that I could finally accept it: *Dee Dee Michaud will not be here tomorrow.*

I was still standing at the window when the lights of the First Citizens Bank blinked on, followed by those at the post office. I realized it must be eight o'clock already. My cup of coffee had grown cold and stale on the windowsill. I felt my eyes water with warm tears as a wave of helplessness overtook me. Even if I could talk her out of it, even if Dee Dee would change her plans, I couldn't save her forever. What would I get? Another week or two? Maybe a month? Then I could visit her at a hospital, tubes running into her body like parasites, her brain fried on whatever painkillers the doctors were pumping into her. "I'm dying, Sammy," she had said to me, that day she asked me to help her. "It's not like it's an original idea, you know. It's been going on for a long time." Maybe. But I knew then that each of us—if we're truly lucky—will only lose one friend like Dee

Dee Michaud in our entire lifetimes. And that was original enough for me. Where would I find the strength to face the rest of my life in Fort Kent, Maine, without her somewhere on the planet, alive and well? Worse yet, where would I find the strength to live with the knowledge that I had helped her end her life?

"Sam?" I turned and saw Trooper standing in the doorway. He came on into the kitchen and stood looking out at the bird feeder.

"You're up early," I said.

"Mom says I don't have to go to school this week," he told me. He unzipped his coat and hoisted it off, hung it over the back of the chair.

"You can help me in the clinic if you'd like," I said. "You know. Something to do." He nodded.

"Mom had oatmeal for breakfast," he said, suddenly pleased.

"And she kept it down?" I asked. Trooper nodded. He said nothing for some time, his eyes watching the black-capped chickadees that bounced from tree branches to the feeder, then back to the branches with sunflower seeds in their beaks. We should all have the grace of chickadees. Then Trooper looked up at me.

"Maybe she's gonna be okay after all, Sam," he said. I took a deep breath, and discovered that breathing actually hurt, so tense were my stomach muscles.

"No, Troop," I said, "she isn't gonna be okay. She's really sick. And she's getting more sick. And your mom doesn't want to leave us all behind without being able to say goodbye. She wants to leave this world on her own terms."

"I bet that's how my dad died," Trooper said. I wanted to scoop him up in my arms at that moment, wanted to shield him in any way I possibly could. This must have been how Dee Dee felt, all those years, when Trooper asked about Bobby. This must have been a steady job. Well, it was *my* job now. "Mom says lots of people get cancer," he added, and I was thankful that his thoughts had moved away from Bobby. There would be many times, in the years that lay ahead, for Trooper to ask me about his father.

"Cancer is a terrible disease, Troop," I said. "It's nobody's fault that they get it. It's just some very bad luck." He went over to the fridge and opened it, found a Coke on the bottom shelf. He had felt at home in this house for some time now, and we could thank Dee Dee for that. He went back to the table and sat down, his can of Coke in front of him. I watched him from the corner of my eye. I thought he was reading words on the can.

"Mom says I'm not gonna get sick," he said finally. And I realized that something else was mixed in with his pain over losing his mother: *guilt*.

"Troop," I said, "you don't need to feel bad that

you're not sick, too. The fact that you're well is what has kept your mom going. You don't need to feel guilt, Troop." He looked up at me with wise, yet innocent eyes, and I could tell that he had needed to hear this from someone other than his mom. Then he went back to staring at the Coke can, satisfied with my answer, at least for the time being. Dee Dee would be proud of me just then. I was learning the difficult task of being a dad.

"There's *high fructose corn syrup* in Coke," Trooper stated matter-of-factly.

"And that's one of the *good* ingredients," I said.

"Canned under authority of the Coca-Cola Company, Atlanta, Georgia," Trooper read on. "By Coca-Cola Bottling Company, Charlotte, North Carolina." He looked up at me, those same innocent eyes. "How come they make it in North Carolina and bottle it in Atlanta?" he asked. I thought about this for a few seconds.

"Trooper," I said, "you should know now that as your newly adopted father there are some questions I'm never going to have the answers to. Not ever. And *that's* one of them." Trooper laughed at this. It had been my greatest talent with his mother, too, making her laugh when she needed to. "Listen," I said. "We need to keep busy today. We're *men,* after all. And men need to do physical things. Why do you think they invented fooze ball? So what do you say? Is there anything you'd like to do for your mom,

something you always intended to do, but didn't?"
Keep him busy, I thought, keep him busy today. Tomorrow it will all be over.

"I could make her a candle," said Trooper. "A
guardian angel to show her the way, you know,
when she dies." I hadn't expected this. How would
candle making keep his mind off Dee Dee? Then, I
understood that it was exactly what he needed to
do. Of course he couldn't forget that his mother was
about to die. But he could do something with his
hands that would make him feel that he had a part
in it all.

"You got it, ace," I said. "Let's make a candle.
Now, how *do* you make a candle?" Trooper smiled.

"I'll show you, Sam," he said. "I'll make a mold
candle. It's easier." I wondered how many of us poor
souls were left in Fort Kent who didn't know how to
make a goddamn candle. I imagined a secret group
meeting in the back room at Bee Jay's Tavern every
Wednesday night, sad and forlorn outcasts: *the
Candle-Challenged Club*.

We found Lydia's candle-making items in her
workroom. Trooper searched through the different
molds that Lydia had bought, molds shaped like
Easter eggs, petaled flowers, molds for floating candles, pear-shaped candles, octagon candles. Where
had I been when she dragged all this stuff into the
house? Trooper finally found the mold he was looking for.

"I wanna make her a star-shaped candle," Trooper said. "I want to make her a candle like the star in Orion's foot." I smiled. Dee Dee had done a good job in teaching Trooper all she could about the world we live in. She'd done a good job, and now it would be up to Lydia and me to do the rest of that job: raise Trooper to manhood. Shape him, layer after layer, until he became a human being who gave something back to the world before he went out. Jesus, I was starting to think like Dee Dee, with all that candle-mania crap.

"Just for the record," I said to Trooper, as we brought the paraffin, the mold, and the double boiler out to the kitchen. "I thought you didn't believe in that candle-as-guardian-angel theory." Trooper shrugged.

"Mom says why take a chance? It just might be true," Trooper answered me. I nodded. That was good enough for me. "First, you fill the mold with water," he said. "That'll tell you how much wax you need. For every three and a half ounces of water, you're gonna need three ounces of cold wax." I was impressed. He sounded like a serious little scientist at work on some important experiment.

"I see," I said. "What now?"

"Now we put the wick through the mold," Trooper said, and he did so, sealing the end of it with mold seal. "Now we need to put stearin, one-tenth the amount of wax, into the mold. That way, the candle will come out easier."

"Sounds good," I said, thinking, *what the hell is stearin?* I watched as he put the paraffin wax into the double boiler. Then we both stood like alchemists of old and waited as the wax melted. When it had, Trooper carefully lifted the top boiler and poured the wax into the star mold.

"You gotta leave about a half inch at the top," he said, a frown knitted between his eyebrows. "Then, after the wax has settled, you gotta tap the side of the mold, to get rid of any air bubbles in there." I watched as he filled a huge bowl with cold water and then placed the mold inside, where it would cool. He looked up at me, his eyes alive with the magical work that had taken place: he'd just made his own candle. To look at his face, one would have thought he'd just turned lead into gold. "In an hour, it'll be ready," he added importantly. I looked down at the star-shaped candle before me, wide at the base, then running up to a narrow peak at the top.

"Rigel," I said to Trooper, and he smiled.

"Rigel," he repeated, looking down at the vanilla-colored star before him. His own creation. His own supernova.

The day wore away in slow seconds. I tried to stay busy at the clinic. Lydia had come to fetch

Trooper. He and Dee Dee were to spend a quiet day together. I tried not to think about the boy, or about Dee Dee, as I flushed mites out of cat ears with Tresaderm; dewormed dogs; cleaned tartar from off feline teeth; and then set the broken wing of an evening grosbeak that Leroy Martin had found lying in the middle of the street, in front of Rose's Dress Shop. Before I knew it, it was 6 P.M. and Lydia had appeared in the doorway of the clinic. Trooper was with her.

"Hey, Dr. Thibodeau," Lydia said. "Dee Dee's asking where you are."

We decided to walk to 204 Bay Street. When I stepped out of the clinic, I was surprised to see that darkness had already enveloped Fort Kent. Our daylight hours were growing more and more brief. On December 21, exactly two weeks away, would come the shortest day of all, the winter solstice, that time when the sun is farthest south of the equator. My shortest day in which to grieve.

As we walked down our street, in the direction of Bay, snow crunched with cold beneath our boots. Most of the houses we passed were already decorated for Christmas. And the lampposts along the streets of town were awash with colored lights and fake holly, the Thanksgiving holiday being the trigger that gets the seasonal ball rolling. It was easy to tell which homes were Franco by the Nativity scenes in the front yards. Over and over again I saw Mary and Joseph, kneeling above the baby Jesus, while around them plastic sheep and cows and mules looked on with wondering eyes.

"Hey," I said to Lydia, and pointed at the animals. "Potential patients. That cow looks like it could use a few liters of calcium." This made her laugh. Trooper had stopped to talk to Randy Cloutier, now his best friend. But he soon caught up behind us, Lancelot playfully biting at the heels of his boots. Now and then he stooped to make a snowball to toss at someone's mailbox. Lydia looked lovely beside me, in the warm blue parka I'd bought for her the previous Christmas, the one Dee Dee had worn to go sliding. I could see Jupiter already appearing low on the horizon, as bright and dazzling as the star in the east. But we weren't three wise men on our way to verify a miraculous birth. We were two small-town vets and a kid, on our way to a *death*.

"Word is out that Dee Dee is checking into the hospital tomorrow," Lydia whispered to me, so that Trooper wouldn't hear. "I told Renée and Patrice to stop by. And a few others from the candle-making class. But I'm worried, Sam. You know what some of the gossips have been saying, that Dee Dee has AIDS, and that they can catch it from her."

"Idiots," I said, anger rising up within me. What made some people so damn *rotten?*

237

"I'm worried that people are too afraid to come by," Lydia added. I said nothing. Human nature had stopped surprising me long ago.

We walked past the library, where Dee Dee had once hidden in the coat closet, when she was not much older than Trooper. The idea was to wait until the library closed for the night, and when it did, she opened the door and let me in. We spent the rest of the evening reading with flashlights. No, not *War and Peace*. Not *A Tale of Two Cities,* but medical books with pictures of male and female organs, accompanied by academic descriptions of *what* to put *where,* and *why,* advice I am still uncertain of to this day. It was most likely written by a sixty-year-old virgin with a Ph.D. in human anatomy. Funny, but back then we thought the greatest mystery of life was sex. It isn't. Death is.

As Lydia and I walked the length of Bay Street, I could almost feel the warmth of a million footsteps buried there in the cement, beneath the blue-white snow of winter. Dee Dee and I had taken our first steps on that street, scraped our knees there, ridden our first bikes, played hopscotch, jumped rope, ridden our last bikes. It was a street alive, breathing with memories. On each side the same houses, except for new coats of paint, still looked out at the street with watchful eyes. Not much had changed, yet *everything* had changed. Trooper caught up to my side, tired of distracting himself with snowballs. He reached up for my hand and I gave it to him. My arm around Lydia, we walked on, like sad paper dolls, linked together and uncertain of our futures.

At 204 Bay, the big front window was ablaze with dancing candlelight. Dee Dee opened her door before we could climb the steps up to the porch and stomp the snow from our feet. She was wearing makeup, I noticed, her eyes looking very exotic in her thin face, a tinge of color applied to her lips. I noticed something else there on her face. Serenity? Resignation? Peace? I understood now what Lydia had tried to tell me the night before. "Dee Dee's ready, Sam," she said. I had tossed and turned all night, falling in and out of sleep, unable to accept the fact that someone as strong as Dee Dee would go willingly. But I saw before me now the face of a woman who had taken up every gauntlet that lay at her feet. She had played every hand, and then she hit a streak of bad luck. That was it. After all, many people die of old age without ever *having lived*.

For an hour we four sat on the floor in the parlor and lingered over old scrapbooks, some Dee Dee's, some my mother's. Then we flipped through yearbooks from Fort Kent High School, dozens of pictures, images of our lives: Dee Dee and I at my third birthday party, the day we met; Dee Dee and I bathing in the galvanized tub; graduating from the eighth grade. Frozen seconds of our lives.

"Look, Trooper," Dee Dee said, wanting him to

239

know all that was possible about her life. "Here is Sammy and me as Humphrey Bogart and Lauren Bacall, at the talent show, when we did a scene from *Key Largo.*" Trooper looked down at the photo for a long time. We were just about his age when it was taken.

"Who's Humphrey Bogart?" he asked. We laughed, but there was a tension in the air that Lydia and I could feel hovering, a palpable strain. I followed her out to the kitchen, under the guise of helping her open a bottle of wine, although I needed a shot of Jack Daniel's more than I had ever needed anything in my life. And I was getting angry.

"Where the hell are Ross and Vickie?" I asked. I could understand small minds like Florence's and Alberta's. But *Ross?* Lydia shrugged, and handed me the corkscrew.

"He'll turn up," she said. I knew she was trying to placate me.

"And where are Patrice and Renée?" She shrugged again.

"I told you I was worried," she said. She went back to the parlor. I picked up the phone and quietly dialed Ross's number. His answering machine clicked on. I hung up. Where was he, for Chrissakes?

In the parlor again, I noticed Trooper sneaking an anxious peek out the front window. I gave Dee Dee her glass of wine and she took it with a steady hand.

"I wonder what wine Martha Stewart would serve on a night like this," Dee Dee said. She was wearing a long denim skirt and a faded denim blouse, the ends tied up in a sturdy blue rose at her stomach. I had never seen her so thin. Her hair was pulled back from her thin face with combs. And I saw that she wore a small heart on a chain around her neck. Even in sickness, even with this disease pulling her down, she still radiated a kind of beauty that is rare. Her soul was shining through loud and clear. The wonder girl of Fort Kent, Maine. Biggest Flirt for four years running.

Dee Dee was getting tired, so Lydia and I helped her over to the sofa. Trooper had gone upstairs for his Instamatic camera. He wanted pictures, he said. So we posed on the sofa for several, Lydia and I taking turns snapping the shots. The clock in the kitchen ticked softly. The house creaked in its bones. The organdy curtains billowed softly in the warm air shooting up from the furnace. *How can people be so cruel?* I wondered. Trooper was at the window again, peering at the street. I knew he was wondering, too.

"Come on," Dee Dee said finally, when it seemed the stillness would crack and break, like glass between us. "This is a party," she said. "I want to see smiles on those faces." In the candlelight, the dark circles under her eyes had disappeared as if by magic.

"Dee Dee," I said. I had made up my mind to say something, about people, about the foibles of human beings. We couldn't go on all night long *pretending*. But I didn't have to say anything. Trooper bounded suddenly from the window.

"Sam!" he yelled. "Come look!" I went to the window. As far as I could see, all the way down Bay Street, dots of fire were bouncing up and down in the night air.

"What the hell is going on?" I asked Trooper. I still couldn't decipher what I was seeing. It looked like hordes of cigarette lighters at a Bruce Springsteen concert. Then I realized what was happening: dozens of flickering candles were bobbing in the darkness. People were coming from up and down the street, people were coming from all over town, to 204 Bay Street, each holding a lighted candle in his or her hands. I saw Ross at the vanguard, with Vickie. As Dee Dee's front yard quickly filled, it looked like a huge field of fireflies lighting up the night. And above the candles were faces of the townspeople: people who knew Dee Dee since she was a little girl; her new friends; her students from the candle-making class; the bartenders at Bee Jay's; the waitresses from the cafe; even strangers. It seemed to me that half of Fort Kent was there. They had come from all over town to say goodbye with their candles, candles they had bought from her. Candles she had taught them how to make. They

242

had come to say goodbye to a wild and crazy girl, a girl they had grown to love.

I helped Dee Dee up from the sofa and over to the door. I wanted her to see the magnificent sight that was unfurling in her front yard on that cold winter's night. Lydia opened the door and now we could hear the murmur of excited voices.

"Oh, Trooper, look," Dee Dee said, and nodded weakly at the sea of candles filling up the front lawn, the driveway, the street out front. Candles everywhere. "Look at all my angels." Her face was radiant. When I put my arms around her—she was light as a wish—I could feel her little heart beating fiercely against my chest. Dee Dee's heart. I couldn't imagine it ever not beating.

"There's Ross!" Trooper said, and pointed at the shaggy head looming above the thin denim jacket. Ross had his back to us, but he was in charge, no doubt about it. He signaled to the crowd, like some kind of bizarre conductor, and suddenly their voices rose together on the cold air, their warm breaths visible above the burning candles. At first, I thought they might sing a Christmas carol, just for Dee Dee. But I should have known better, not with Ross Cloutier as organizer. Ross had sung "My Ding-a-Ling" at his sister's wedding. Instead, Ross had them sing the very first song that the Acute Angles had ever learned, an Oldie but Goodie by the Temptations:

I got sunshine, on a cloudy day,
And when it's cold outside, I got the month of May,
I guess you'll say, what can make me feel this way?
My girl, talking 'bout my girl, my girl . . .

I stood there grinning like a Cheshire cat. In my parents' day you might have heard "Amazing Grace" or "Old Rugged Cross" at such a somber event as this, saying goodbye to a loved one forever. Not at 204 Bay Street, not on that night. But what do you expect from a bunch of leftover hippies and full-fledged baby boomers?

"That was the first song we ever learned, Sam," Dee Dee said. I nodded. I don't think anything could have made her happier. I vowed right then and there that I would buy Ross Cloutier every beer he could ever want for the rest of his life, at Bee Jay's Tavern, on those nights when he and I would go there, in those years that lay ahead in our future, nights when Dee Dee's ghost would move through our minds like a cool wind. Dee Dee's *ghost*.

"Happy Pearl Harbor Day," I told her, just as Ross stepped up onto the porch and gave her a gentle hug of his own.

"Here," he said. "A bunch of us chipped in for this." He handed her a Polaroid picture, and Dee Dee took it, peered down at it with great interest. Leaning over her shoulder, I saw that it was a picture of a new tile on Bee Jay's ceiling, one right next to mine, above the big table in front of the fireplace, our fa-vorite spot: *Bay Street Candles,* it read. *Dee Dee Michaud, Owner & Candle Maker.* Someone had drawn a beautifully tapered candle, in a lovely holder, its flame flickering eternally. Beneath the can-dle were the words: *I shall be a candle-holder, and look on. Shakespeare.*

"Oh, my God!" Dee Dee said. "I finally made Bee Jay's ceiling!" Ross beamed to see her so happy. The words couldn't have been more appropriate, or so I thought as I looked out at all the human *candle-holders* filling up the yard. I would need to remember, for Trooper's sake, that there are so many people on this planet who make up for the Florences and Albertas. I would need to remember this.

The night was ending too fast. I had helped Dee Dee back to the sofa and made her comfortable there. Faces filed in and out of the parlor, folks say-ing goodbye to Dee Dee, some promising to come visit her in the hospital later on. And then the voices dwindled, the house grew quiet again, the candles burning lower. It was time to begin the longest good-bye of our lives. We left Dee Dee with Trooper, alone in the parlor, and when he emerged again he seemed calm, quiet, resigned himself. I knew it wouldn't always be that way. I knew there would be nights when he wouldn't sleep, days in class when he couldn't concentrate, lonely times when he'd miss her until his heart might break. My job as his new father was to help him past those times, and, in doing so, get past them myself. Vickie and Ross said their own goodbyes to Dee Dee. Then, with Trooper between them, they took him back to his new home, above the Northern Maine Veterinary Clinic, until he and Lydia and I moved out to our new house on Gagnon Road, in the spring, and set about filling that home with memories of our own.

I poured myself another glass of wine while Lydia gave Dee Dee her last sponge bath and then helped her into the long flannel nightgown. It had belonged to her mother, and Dee Dee wanted to wear it. It was only ten o'clock, but Dee Dee was tired. As loving as the evening had been, it had been difficult for her. As I flipped slowly through the pages of that day's *Bangor Daily News,* not really reading the items, just needing to do something with my hands, Lydia appeared in the door of the parlor, a soft smile on her face. I was beginning to feel that everyone was in on some cosmic secret, a font of serenity to which I had no access. Lydia took her blue parka from off the coatrack at the door.

"I'm going for a little walk," she said. "To clear my head. You and Dee Dee spend some time together." I watched the blue parka disappear out the door. And for the second time that week I wondered how I had been so lucky to find Lydia Newhart in this ocean of five billion people.

246

When I went into the parlor I saw Trooper's candle, the one he had made for Dee Dee just that morning, burning on the table. I smiled, pointed at it.

"I see he gave it to you," I said. Dee Dee nodded. She was sitting in the big lounge chair by the window, in her mother's flannel gown, her feet up on the footrest.

"He told me it would be my guardian angel," she said. "He told me my guardian angel would show me the way up to heaven." She stated this as a fact, without sadness or remorse. I went over and stood by the window. I could see Lydia's silhouette just turning the corner.

"Tell me the truth," I said. "Do you really believe all that talk about candles being angels? Do you really believe in things you can't see?" Dee Dee lay her head back, against the neck rest, and looked over at me. I had only been teasing her, but she seemed to be thinking deeply about my question before she answered.

"I believe in *spring*," she said finally. "Even though it's winter right now, and I can't see the buds on the wild cherry. Or fields full of sweet clover. Or warblers building their nests. I can't see spring right now, with all this snow, but I still believe in it, Sammy."

"Good answer," I said, and was surprised that the words came out without the sarcasm I had intended. I stood for a long time looking over at her face. In the candlelight, she had grown beautiful again, Dee Dee and her magical candles. She stared back, waiting for me to speak. I cleared my throat.

"Does this mean I'm never gonna get to sleep with you?" I asked. When she laughed, it was the old laugh, the one that rolls up from your gut, pure laughter, the way she *used* to laugh. That was my greatest talent when it came to Dee Dee Michaud: I could make her laugh like no one else could, not Bobby Langford, not Lydia, not Ross, not anybody.

"Oh, Sammy," Dee Dee said then. "God, but I have loved you." I went over and sat on the floor by her chair. She reached out a thin hand to touch my hair. I smiled as I felt her slowly curling strands around the tips of her fingers. That's what she always did to Trooper. "You have been my friend," she said, "and you have been my brother. I would trust my son to no one but you." I reached up and took her little hand.

"You were my first love," I told her. She nodded.

"I know," she said, and smiled.

"You know?" I asked.

"Of course," said Dee Dee. "Girls know stuff like that."

"Well, just between you and me," I said, "I'm sick of hearing about female powers. Trooper is sick of it, too."

"Get used to it," said Dee Dee. It was my turn to smile.

"What else do you know?" I asked.

248

"The day of our graduation," Dee Dee said, "when we were sitting in your car. Just before I showed you my engagement ring." I remembered that day all too well.

"What about it?"

"You were going to ask me to go steady," she said. I couldn't have been more surprised. I had never let her know how I felt. I had called her *nitwit,* and *idiot,* and *monkey,* and every name as far from a *dearism* as I could get.

"You knew?" I asked. This amused her further. The way Lydia had been amused that night when Dee Dee and Trooper had come over for dinner, when she teased me about my crush on Dee Dee. The night I learned about Freddy Stolinski. The son of a bitch, whoever he was.

"Sammy," she said, "don't you realize how special our relationship has been? It's lasted all these years. Longer than my marriage to Bobby. Longer than Ross's marriage. And it will last forever. If we had been lovers it would have been over years ago." She lay back again, resting. "We're Scarlett and Rhett, baby. We're Bogey and Bacall. And it doesn't get any better than that." I reached into my shirt pocket. I had something I wanted to give her. I'd spent almost two days searching among the boxes in my attic but I had finally found it. As I took it from my pocket, the green stone caught the flickering light of the candles. *Class of 1982,* it said. *Fort Kent High School.* My old class ring. Dee Dee beamed as I held it up for her to see.

"Dee Dee Michaud," I said, and took her pale hand back into my own. "Will you go steady with me?" I saw her eyes glisten.

"I thought you'd never ask," she said. So I carefully pushed my class ring onto her ring finger. Dee Dee held her hand up before her so that she could see the stone.

"Kiss me, Sammy," she said. And I remembered the twelve-year-old face, that day on the riverbank, that day I knew I'd love her forever. I leaned forward and kissed her softly on the lips.

"Here's looking at you, kid," I said. Maybe it was her voice, fragile and lilting against the stillness of the big house. Maybe it was the candlelight, soft and forgiving, as yellow as those old days of summer. Whatever it was, a great blanket of peace settled down over me just then, as though it were a sprinkling of warm water. I felt so acutely *alive,* so in touch with every cell within myself. It was the same special feeling that I'd felt that night in Quebec City, as the sun rose over the St. Lawrence, Dee Dee and I the only two left awake, a *prickling* sensation almost. As if all our cells had suddenly risen up to remind us that we were very much alive. The electricity of life. That's what I was feeling now.

We were still holding hands when Lydia returned.

"I'll make up the bed," Lydia offered. Together,

she and I opened the sofa bed. I waited as Lydia brought clean sheets down from upstairs and quickly made it up. Then I helped Dee Dee from her chair and over to the bed. Lydia and I positioned her beneath the blankets as best we could. Funny, but even then, even with peace settled into my gut, I still had hope. That old phone call at the last minute: the governor's pardon. But Dee Dee hadn't changed her mind. As I fitted the pillow behind her head, she began to cough, so long and hard that I thought she would never be able to stop. When she finally did, she looked up at me, determined.

"It's time, Sammy," she said, and I nodded. I couldn't fail her now. Lydia went to the kitchen and in a few minutes was back with a cup of tea and a slice of toast. Food for Dee Dee's empty stomach. I tore the bread into bite-size pieces for her. She chewed slowly, taking small sips of the tea. When she finished, she took the Dramamine, to keep her stomach as steady as possible. I looked at my watch. In an hour, if she still wanted to go through with this, she could take the pills. I felt my own stomach churning, the tension growing into a neat fist, all the peacefulness slipping away. *Stay strong,* I told myself. *Don't break down now.* Lydia came back with a bottle of wine and poured a glass for me and one for herself. We sat sipping our wine, in the room shimmering with candles. Dee Dee spoke first.

"Trooper has a spelling test next week," she said.

"He'll need help." Her voice was so tiny that it sounded like the voice locked in a gramophone. Lydia nodded.

"He'll get a hundred," I said. "I'll work with him."

"He spells like I do," Dee Dee whispered. Her forehead was covered with beads of glistening sweat. Lydia went for a damp cloth and came back and wiped Dee Dee's forehead with it.

"There was so much excitement today," said Lydia. "You're worn out."

"It was worth it," Dee Dee whispered. "I'm on Bee Jay's ceiling." Then: "Is it time yet?" Lydia looked at the clock. It was. Almost an hour had drifted its way through our lives. *Remember this,* I told myself. *Don't forget this lesson. Remember how precious every second of life can be.*

"Listen," Dee Dee said, "when he's old enough, tell Trooper the truth. Tell him everything about Bobby. Tell him about this night. Kids need the truth. When he's old enough, Sam."

"Dee Dee," I said, "please understand that I have to say this. You can change your mind, sweetie. It's not too late." She nodded.

"I know," she said. "But it's time, Sammy. It's time for me to go."

Lydia came back with five of the morphine pills. The other nine she had already ground up and mixed into some yogurt, which she carried in a bowl. I poured Dee Dee a glass of wine. How could I have ever known, on all those partying nights of our senior year, that the day would come when I would pour Dee Dee Michaud a glass of wine because the alcohol would double the toxicity of the morphine? I helped Dee Dee sit up on the sofa bed. Then she reached a frail hand for the glass of wine. I gave it to her. She looked at Lydia.

"I'll take the pills alone," she whispered. "Like we planned."

"No," I said, surprised at the sound of my own voice. "I'm not leaving you." I sat down on the edge of her bed, and Lydia sat next to me. I felt a rush of love for her just then. My wife. My companion. For better or worse. At my side. Even through this. Dee Dee looked at us. She knew I meant what I said.

"Lyddie," she said. "Just Sammy, okay?" Their eyes locked for a second, but I could tell that they had exchanged a million words in that one look. Lydia came and knelt next to the bed, took Dee Dee's hand, put it up to her lips and kissed it.

"Goodbye, precious," said Lydia. "Knowing you has been a great gift." Dee Dee smiled.

"My soul sister," she said, and Lydia nodded. She stood, touched a hand to my shoulder, as if to give me strength, and then left the room. *Dee Dee and Lydia.* How had such a regular, nonspiritual, run-of-the-mill veterinarian like me, of average height and looks, ever been so blessed as to have had them *both* in my life?

"Good thing you didn't tell her we're going steady," I said to Dee Dee. And there it was again, that old fire in her eyes, a fire deeper than the reflection of all her candles. It was her *soul,* that's what I saw, Dee Dee Michaud's precious soul, whatever that may be. What can I say about her? What will I say to Trooper, when the day comes and he asks about this night? *She wasn't afraid,* that's what I'll say. *She wasn't even beaten by the disease. She was a girl who always swung for the bleachers in the ninth inning. She was Dee Dee Michaud as I always knew her. She was in charge.*

Dee Dee motioned for me to pass her the pills. I did so, and she swallowed them, drinking as much of the wine as she could. Then she reached for the yogurt. We knew she had to eat it quickly.

"Will you sing to me, Sammy?" she asked. That little smile again on her face. I nodded.

"Does it have to be something by AƂBA?"

"No," she said, "but you have to promise to put the poster up at your clinic."

I watched as she ate the yogurt. She'd been having difficulty in swallowing for some days now, but she managed to get it down. It held the last of the pulverized pills. She sipped more wine—this would wash it down, soften the bitter taste—and then she lay back against the pillow. I stretched out at her side on the bed, took her tiny hand in mine. Lydia had lit all the candles in the parlor, as Dee Dee had requested: candles of all shapes and sizes, candles everywhere—pear-shaped, flower-shaped, floating candles, candles that looked like seashells, candles that smelled of vanilla; the room seemed on fire with them. Dee Dee's eyes watched the dancing flickers.

"I wonder if heaven is this bright," she whispered. I brought her hand up to my face, held it there.

"It will be when *you* get there," I told her. I knew the pills wouldn't take long, if she could just hold them down.

"Sing to me, Sammy," she said again. So, in that room of dancing fire, I sang to Dee Dee Michaud, the first girl I had ever loved.

"I got sunshine, on a cloudy day, and when it's cold out-side, I got the month of May, I guess you'll say, what can make me feel this way, my girl, talking 'bout my girl."

Minutes slipped away before Dee Dee spoke again. "Bobby," she suddenly whispered. She had pushed up on her elbows and was staring at the star-shaped candle Trooper had made for her. "Bobby?" Her stare was so fixed, so directed, that I knew she was certain she saw someone standing there. But there was no one. Just the candle on a small table, and behind it, in the background, the organdy curtains of the parlor window. But Dee Dee smiled anyway, her eyes on something I could not see, could not envision, not yet anyway. And it was then that I knew Dee Dee was ready to let go. This time, I was even glad that Bobby Langford, Trooper's good-looking father, might be there to show her the way. *The World's Biggest Ball of Twine. The World's Largest Cowboy Boot.*

Dee Dee relaxed again, back against the pillow, her eyes still open, still on whatever she saw.

"I got sunshine, on a cloudy day," I sang again, my eyes weltering with tears, *"and when it's cold outside, I got the month of May, I guess you'll say, what can make me feel this way, my girl, talking 'bout my girl."*

And then she was gone. She had slipped away like a prayer. I knew this because I felt a jolt of electricity race through her fingers, so strong that my hand tingled with the force of it. I looked in her eyes, still wide open, and I saw that the fire, too, was gone. It had left her. It was her soul, whatever a soul may be, Dee Dee Michaud's soul leaving her cold and useless and sick body, rising up over all those brilliant candles, rising up and going off I didn't know where. Maybe into that bright star at Orion's foot. I reached over and gently closed her eyes.

"Lyddie?" I said. She heard me and came down the long hallway and into the parlor. She said nothing, just came and lay down on the other side of the bed. She put her head on Dee Dee's chest, reached for her other hand. And the two of us—my wife and I—held Dee Dee Michaud close to us, until all the candles burned low.

. . .

256

It had started to snow by the time Lydia and I walked home that night, away from the stillness of the house at 204 Bay Street, light feathery flakes. I stood for a moment and looked back at the dark parlor window behind us. This house would be Trooper's house one day. Dee Dee had seen to it. Maybe he would fall in love with this little town, and it will pull him back to it, no matter where he travels. Maybe, in his adult years, he will come to raise his family in that house. Maybe he will grow up to be like me, the kind of man who stays close to hearth and kin. Maybe he will sense, too, that there's something in this northern Maine soil that holds us firmly to it.

We walked on, Lydia and I, the cold snow breaking beneath our boots, the only sounds in Fort Kent, except for the whine of a truck shifting gears somewhere down on Charette Hill. I reached for Lydia's hand. Our puffs of warm breath hung like dreamy clouds on the winter's air, like our futures, small orbits spinning ahead of us. The streetlights on the Canadian side were twinkling like scattered diamonds. It was just an hour before dawn. Venus had already pushed her way across the dark sky, and now she hung there like a sparkling Christmas ornament. I stopped walking and scanned the sky overhead until I found Orion, the great hunter. His sword was still raised, still ready for battle, his brilliant belt still buckled. And there at his toe: Rigel, his brightest and best star. That's when I knew.

"I'm going to write this down," I said to Lydia. "I'm going to write down Dee Dee's story. For Trooper."

And then we walked on, toward the rest of our lives.

ACKNOWLEDGMENTS

Tom Viorikic, the first reader.

My niece Dr. Diana "Dee Dee" Pelletier of Goodlettesville Animal Hospital, here in Tennessee, for her veterinarian information. I named Dee Dee Michaud (pronounced *me-show*) after Diana. And thanks to Dr. John Parker, for all the equine lore.

To veterinarians the world over, who rarely receive the money or respect they deserve. And to Walden's Puddle, in Joelton, Tennessee, for their work with wild animals.

Dr. Charles Blanke, at Vanderbilt University Clinic, for his kind assistance, and his sharing of much needed information.

Dr. Sam Pelletier, formerly of Fort Kent. Although I have never met him, I am such a fan of Sammy

259

Pelletier, the athlete and former West Point captain, that I wanted to name the main character in this book "Sammy Pelletier." But Pelletier, a common name in Franco-Maine, is my own last name. When Sammy Pelletier won the Philadelphia Marathon in 1983, I kept his success in mind as I chugged my six miles each day, finally reaching a personal best of 6:32. (Sammy walks his dog faster than that.) Now an optometrist in York, Maine, Sam gave me permission over the phone to use his name in this book. (I still run daily, to the mailbox.)

Edith Thibodeau Pelletier, my grandmother, in memory of her thick French accent and her broken English, a poetry I miss deeply. I gave Sam Thibodeau, the main character in this book, her family name.

John Hafford, also from northern Maine and owner of Northland Studio, in Caribou. John did the wonderful artwork. Thanks also to his wife, Jessie Masse, for her valuable input.

Arlene Friedman. Thank you. Thank you. Thank you.

Pat Mulcahy, my editor, and the following folks at Doubleday: Denell Downum, Amy King, Carol Lazare, Robin Swados, Paula Breen, Kathy Hale, and Gerry Triano.

Naomi Nicolas, at the University of Maine at Fort Kent, for her indispensable help.

Shelley Liles and Karen Essex, who are coming

from Nashville to visit Fort Kent and see for themselves. (Sherry Sullivan and I are the official guides.) Here's to our wilderness stay at Round Pond, Maine, and to Dana Shaw, Barry Ouellette, and Marilyn Daily for their kind hospitality.

Jim Glaser, Sherry Sullivan, Tamara Saviano, Eliza Clark, and Peggy Walton-Walker, for being supportive friends.

Stephanie Germain, my fingers are crossed.

Paul, Sue, and Ashley Gauvin, of Mankins, Texas, whose dog, Cody, was run down and killed by a mindless redneck who thinks he's a cowboy. Cody lives again in this book.

Last, but certainly not least, I want to thank the following people and businesses of Fort Kent, Maine, who allowed me to use their names in this little book (I wonder how many times we've all sung "The French Song"?): Lise Boucher and Rita Canaan (Bee Jay's Tavern); Larry and Judy Fitzherbert; Billy Caron; Alain Ouellette; Mike Taggett (who actually teaches math, and owns no cows); Mike Hafford (of Allagash); Andrew Jackson (formerly of Allagash); Jim Desjardins; Lisa Ornstein; Nick Hawes; Sue Roy; Naomi and Danny Nicholas; Julia Bayly (*St. John Valley Times*); Joan St Amant; Diane Morneault (and the band High Fidelity); Bennett Pelletier; Ann Gendreau; Arms Nadeau (Nadeau's House of Furniture); Vernon Pelletier; Fred Malmborg (my teacher who encouraged me to write, but who owns no goat);

Louie Pelletier (who owns no auto repair); Mrs. Robichaud (in honor of Doris Robichaud Lazarre, now of Bristol, Connecticut); Lana Pelletier (who couldn't mend a bicycle seat if she tried); Warren Harvey (Radio Shack); Uncle Earl O'Leary; Jacques, Luc, André Michel, Philippe, and Sophie Ouellette, for letting me use their golden retriever's name (Swede) as well as his memory; Connie, Tracey, Doreen, and Stacey, at Shear Perfection; Leroy Martin; Chamberlain's Grocery (actually in Cross Rock, Maine); Thibodeau's Insurance; Quigley's; Pelletier Florist; Rose's Dress Shop (officially McLellan's); Paradis Shop & Save; Rick Levasseur (now in Bangor); Louise's Magic Mirror; Laverdiere's Drug (now called Rite Aid); Country Cottage (with new owners Laurel and Priscilla Daigle—goodbye, Giselle); Century Theatre, on Hall Street; Bouchard's Car Sales (Gilman Bouchard, Inc.); Doris's Cafe (where you can order ployes); Sirois' Restaurant; Claude's Restaurant; First Citizen's Bank; China Garden; Caroll's Sunoco (now Fort Kent Irving). And Sherry Sullivan, of Bangor, who loves Fort Kent as much as I do.

P.S.: Hello, Spencer Brydon.

And don't miss . . .

DANCING AT THE HARVEST MOON

by K. C. McKinnon

Forty-five-year-old Maggie McIntyre has been abandoned by her husband for a much younger woman. She finds some old letters in the attic from the first love in her life as they remind her of the precious summers she spent at the Harvest Moon dance hall so many years ago.

Now she is returning to the peace of the northern wilderness Little Bear Lake, hoping to recapture the woman she once was and the woman she knows she could be again. Time has changed the place she knew—until a second chance at love makes an unexpected appearance. . . .

Published by Ballantine Books.
Available wherever books are sold.

Want to know a secret?
It's sexy, informative, fun, and FREE!!!

❧ PILLOW TALK ❧

Join Pillow Talk and get advance information and sneak peeks at the best in romance coming from Ballantine. All you have to do is fill out the information below!

♥ My top five favorite authors are: _____

_____

_____

_____

_____

♥ Number of books I buy per month: ❑ 0-2 ❑ 3-5 ❑ 6 or more

♥ Preference: ❑ Regency Romance ❑ Historical Romance
     ❑ Contemporary Romance ❑ Other

♥ I read books by new authors: ❑ frequently ❑ sometimes ❑ rarely

Please print clearly:
Name _____

Address _____

City/State/Zip_____

(Program available to North American residents only, and only while Pillow Talk program continues.)

Don't forget to visit us at
www.randomhouse.com/BB/loveletters

mckinnon

PLEASE SEND TO: PILLOW TALK/
BALLANTINE BOOKS, 11B
1540 BROADWAY
NEW YORK, NY 10036
OR FAX TO PILLOW TALK, 212/782-8442